# Bridget Wilder
# Spy to the Rescue

## Jonathan Bernstein

KATHERINE TEGEN BOOKS
An Imprint of HarperCollins Publishers

Katherine Tegen Books is an imprint of HarperCollins Publishers.

Bridget Wilder: Spy to the Rescue
Copyright © 2016 by Jonathan Bernstein
address HarperCollins Children's Books, a division of HarperCollins
Publishers, 195 Broadway, New York, NY 10007.
www.harpercollinschildrens.com

Library of Congress Control Number: 2015947550
ISBN 978-0-06-238269-6

16 17 18 19 20   CG/RRDH   10 9 8 7 6 5 4 3 2 1
❖
First Edition

To my family

# I Am Not a Spy

"I am not a spy," I say with what I hope is the right mixture of innocence, irritation, and confusion.

The six cheerleaders who kidnapped me regard me with cold, hostile, disbelieving eyes.

If I was any sort of spy, I would not have been so easily bamboozled by the tall, willowy blond girl who sidled up to me as I was heading home from Reindeer Crescent Middle School and held a tiny, big-eyed kitten out under my nose.

"Isn't he beautiful?" the willowy blonde said in a baby voice. "Isn't he the most adorable ball of fluff you've ever seen?"

As if on cue, the little gray kitten reached out a paw to me.

"He loves you," the blond girl almost sang. "He wants to go home with you. Here. Nuzzle him."

My gurgly-voiced new friend thrust the kitten into my hands. Feeling him squirm and adjust himself in my grip made me melt a little inside.

"Take him home," urged the blonde. "Be good to him. Give him the love he needs. He'll give it back to you a hundred times over."

There were a million reasons to say no. My mom hates cats. My dad is allergic. My brother can't be trusted not to sit on them. It would immediately fall in love with my little sister and ignore me. I'd have to feed him and clean up after him, but . . . those big eyes . . . the way he smooshes up against me. The thought hit me: Am I a cat person? I think I am!

I nodded at the blonde. She let out a sigh of contentment, hooked her arm through mine, and guided me toward a school bus parked a few yards away from the others.

"Jump in here and I'll give you his collar and his toys and then this wonderful kitten will be all yours."

*In there?* I should have said. *Why are a cat's collar and toys in a school bus?* I should have said. *By the way, who are you, tall, willowy blond girl?* I should have said. But I was fully focused on the little gentleman squirming in my arms as I climbed the steps into the bus.

The second I was inside, my spy senses clicked into gear. This bus was no refuge for abandoned cats. It was filled with cheerleaders. There were six of them, including the willowy blonde who had lured me onto the bus, all dressed in little pleated skirts and tight blue crop tops bearing the Bronze Canyon Valkyries logo, all displaying enviable abs, all looking like they wanted to rip my head off.

The bus door closed behind me.

"Hit it!" snarled the blonde.

The occupant of the driver's seat, a horse-faced woman somewhere in her late twenties, pulled the bus away from the school.

"Give me that," said the blonde as she yanked the kitten from me.

I sized up the situation. The no-longer-baby-voiced blonde stroked the mewling kitten and barred the door. The other five cheerleaders stood in what I would later discover to be bowling-pin formation in the aisle, making escape impossible.

"Where are we going?"

"Santa Clarita," growled the driver. "To Bronze

Canyon Academy. The school you tried to blackmail."

"I what?" I said, nonplussed.

The girl at the tip of the formation—or the pin-head girl, as I like to think of her—the one with blinding white teeth and hair tied up in a huge polka-dotted bow, thrust her phone in my face. I saw cheerleaders flipping and tumbling. To be more specific, I saw Reindeer Crescent's own Cheerminator squad filmed, in somewhat shaky fashion, mid-practice.

I darted a glance out the window nearest me. The bus was traveling in the opposite direction of my route home.

A finger snapped in my face. "Hey!" barked Big Bow. "Eyes on the screen." I felt a thin wire of anger begin to pulse in me. I looked back at the phone, which now displayed an email. I had to lean so close to read it my glasses almost touched the screen. But I managed to make out the text:

**Pay me $1200 & you'll get the rest of the choreography b4 the Cheerminators premiere it at Classic Cheer.**

The bus juddered around a corner. I stumbled forward, almost falling into Big Bow. She took a step back. The two rows of Valkyries behind her stepped back at the same time. I grabbed on to a seat to get my balance.

"Ladies," I said, trying to remain calm, "I think there's been a mistake. What's going on here is cheer business, and even if being an awesome judge of character isn't a required Valkyrie skill, if you spend a quarter of a second looking at me, it ought to be blindingly clear, I don't care about cheer business."

"Your name does," said one of the mid-pin girls.

Once again, I was forced to squint at the screen. The email was sent by someone known as Weird Debt Girl.

"Don't cheereotype us," said Big Bow. "Being an awesome judge of character is a required Valkyrie skill. In fact, we look for a whole range of talents. One of which is the ability to rearrange letters to form other words."

"Anagrams," I said.

"Cheerleaders love anagrams," she declared. "For instance, if you rearrange the letters of Weird Debt Girl, you get . . ."

"Bridget Wilder." I nodded. "You also get Blew Dried Grit, Bed Dig Twirler, Bridled Wet Rig, and Brr Weed Dig Lit." I used to be very into making anagrams of my name before I was cool like I am now. (My record was two hundred. I know there's a lot more.)

"But mainly you get Bridget Wilder," scowled Big Bow. She folded her arms in triumph. Behind her, the two rows of Valkyries folded their arms in unison.

"You think I sent you an email demanding money for footage of the new Cheerminator choreography?"

The Valkyries nodded in unison.

"Motive!" shouted the willowy blonde. "Your sister's a new Cheerminator."

This was true. My younger sister, Natalie had, on a whim, tried out for the Cheerminators a month earlier, and like the effortless overachiever and automatic center of attention she is, instantly became the high-flying jewel in its crown.

"You conspired with her to cut out the competition," accused Big Bow.

"You're a spy for the Cheerminators," said the driver. "You're trying to get us to buy the footage and then you'll report us to the Cheer Classic competition committee and get us disqualified for contravening the rules."

"I am not a spy," I say.

**Which is where** we came in.

"Only someone who is a spy would say something like that," yells the willowy blonde. She takes the kitten's paw and claws the air with it. "This cat hates you."

"I'm being set up," I tell the Valkyries. "I didn't send the email. I didn't film the practice. I don't want your money."

"What do you think, Coach?" Big Bow calls over to the driver. "She made a pretty convincing case. Should we turn around and take her back to her school?"

The driver taps her fingers off her chin. "Mmmmm . . . ," she ponders. "No."

Big Bow puts a hand on my shoulder and goes to shove me down in the nearest seat. "Relax, Bridget Wilder. You're going to be here for a while. We're taking you back to our school. You're going to confess in front of the entire faculty and student body so that they know our cheer-tegrity is intact!"

"Shouldn't that be cheer-tact?" I ask. Big Bow acts like she didn't hear me.

I make a quick scan of the bus. Blonde and kitty still blocking the front door. Bowling-pin formation stands between me and the rear exit. That leaves windows to my right and left. Am I fast and limber enough to jump toward them, open the locks, and slide out?

You never know if you don't try.

I leap to my left, slither nimbly across the seats, unlock the window, jump up and . . .

. . . Big Bow grabs my ankle and yanks me back.

"Uh-uh, Weird Debt Girl," she mocks. "You're not going anywhere."

I grope for the window but I clutch only air. What a tragic difference from the days when I was the proud owner of a nano-tracksuit and sneakers that enabled me to run like the wind. As Big Bow drags me across the seat, my face makes contact with an unearthly stink. My mind immediately goes to the many butts this seat has supported over the years. I try to think about something less gruesome. Sadly, I can't.

As Big Bow thwarts my big escape plan, the rest of her squad accompanies my defeat with an impromptu cheer session.

"We are the Valkyries and we wanna win!"

*Clap-clap.*

"We murdered you before, watch us kill you again!"

*Clap-clap.*

Big Bow chants along with her spirit sisters while dragging me across the seats. I'm not a regular bus rider but one thing I know: however gross the seats may be, what lurks underneath them is far, far worse.

While Big Bow chants along with her crew, I summon up inner courage and shove my hand under the school bus seat.

"You're old and slow, we're young, fresh, and fast."

*Clap-clap.*

My trembling fingers make contact with something both hard and soft. I resist the urge to gag.

"And we might just decide to stomp all over your . . ."

I wrench the foreign object from under the seat; then I twist around and hurl it straight into the open mouth of Big Bow.

I think it's a black banana but, thank God, I'm not close enough to find out. I am, however, close enough to see the expression on Big Bow's face.

Her eyes widen. She goes bright red. She makes a noise that sounds a bit like *pwah-pwah-pwah*. And she doubles over, coughing and spitting and dry-heaving.

The rest of the Valkyries flock around her, rubbing her back and making sympathetic clucking noises. The willowy blonde puts the kitten up on her shoulder while she ministers to her traumatized teammate.

I pull myself upright and start leaping over the seats. No tracksuit but still nimble! I'm less confident I can squeeze out the window but I know I can kick my way through the rear exit.

Fast as I am, the Valkyries are faster.

One girl from the back pin does handsprings down the aisle of the bus. She lands in a standing position. A second back-pin girl climaxes her handspring by leaping up on the first girl's shoulders. She has to bow her head to avoid banging it on the bus roof but it's an impressive display. Both Valkyries smirk at me. Instinct makes me whirl around.

I see the two mid-pin girls kicking up their legs in the air in perfect time. I do not want one of those flying feet connecting with my face. The Valkyries have boxed me off. I don't have the time or the stomach to search for another black banana. Instead, I squeeze out of my shoes and charge toward the high-kicking duo.

At the exact moment their legs go up in the air, I let myself fall backward as far as I can go without actually slipping over, and I slide straight through their legs.

"Get her!" scream the mid-pin kickers.

My blond friend looks up from the still *pwah-pwah-pwah*-ing Big Bow. I slide toward her, pull myself upright, and snatch the gray kitten off her shoulder.

"She's got Boots!" shrieks the blonde.

"NOOOOOOO!" chorus the Valkyries as one.

"Let me out or the kitten gets it," I say while stroking the cute little fellow to stop his trembling.

The Valkyries gasp in unison. Some of them start to cry.

"Don't hurt him," begs the blonde.

"You were going to hurt me," I point out.

"You're a . . . ," she starts.

"I'm not," I yell in her big dumb face. "I'm not a spy. I'm not a blackmailer. Someone set me up."

"You can tell it to the Classic Cheer committee,"

shouts the coach as she picks up speed. I look out the window. We're on Interstate 5 and she's driving faster.

"Let me off at the next exit or it's curtains for the kitten," I warn her.

"Cheering is more important than kittens," the coach growls back at me. I hear more Valkyries sobbing behind me.

"Let her go, Coach," begs the blonde. "I think she's telling the truth."

"You're cut from the squad," spits the coach. "Traitor."

Okay. Here's the scenario. I'm stuck on a school bus headed to Santa Clarita, some five hours away from my home, with a bunch of emotionally damaged cheerleaders and their demented coach, who clearly is not about to set me free. As I see it, I have only one option. I start to run down the aisle toward the rear exit.

# CHAPTER TWO

# The Setup

"Don't let her go or you're all cut," the coach screams. I hear the thunder of feet pounding after me. I scramble to unlock the rear door of the school bus. Fresh air—well, fresher than the unpleasant bus odor—hits me in the face.

Directly ahead of me, I see a Toyota Sienna minivan driven by a woman who looks surprised to see me emerge from the back of the bus. She looks even more surprised when I jump from the bus, still clinging onto the kitten, who is now taking an adorable little nap—at least, I hope he's napping!—and land stomach-first on the hood of her vehicle.

"Sorry," I say, our faces separated only by an inch of windshield.

I glance over my shoulder and see the other Valkyries clustered around the rear exit. They seem to be debating which one of them should come after me. They're all certainly limber enough to make the leap, but none of them are crazy enough.

Advantage Team Wilder.

The woman driving the Toyota honks her horn and gestures at me to get off. I brandish Boots the kitten, wave his paw at her, and make an *aww* face.

"So cute!" I shout.

In the back of the woman's car, I see two little kids, a boy and a girl, pointing.

"Kitty!" they shriek.

They wave at me and Boots. Mostly Boots. The woman rolls her eyes. Aha! She's a weary mom. Her kids will drive her insane if they don't get to pet the kitten. I gesture to her to open the passenger door.

"I'm a kidnap victim," I yell over the wind. "You have to help me." I hold the sleeping kitten up so her kids get a clear view. "He's a kidnap victim, too!" (Obviously I refrain from pointing out that I'm Boots's kidnapper.)

The woman, who looks as if she's reached the point in life where she just goes along with whatever it throws at her, reaches over and opens the door. I glance back at the gaggle of Valkyries still debating whether or not to pursue me.

"I didn't do it," I bawl back at them. "But I'm going to find out who did!"

I swing into the front passenger seat and toss Boots into the arms of the screaming children.

"Take me back to Reindeer Crescent and he's all yours," I tell the woman.

**The woman drops** me off at Reindeer Crescent Middle School. I wave to Boots as her Toyota drives away, and then I begin my walk home. Obviously I have a lot to think about. My Valkyrie abduction. My daring escape. The mysterious enemy who set me up. Whether I'm really a cat person. And my status as a spy.

I am not currently a spy. It might not even be wholly accurate to say I was ever really a spy. What I was, was bait. Bait for Section 23, a covert agency buried deep inside the bowels of the CIA. I was dangled in front of a former agent who had disappeared into the shadows, the legendary Carter Strike. My biological father. In order to lure Carter Strike back into their grasp and keep their hideous secrets safe, Section 23's devious leader, Brian Spool, bamboozled me.

He smartly played on the insecurity of an adopted

middle child—me!—struggling for attention in a busy family where the effortless overachiever sister and the trouble-magnet brother soaked up every ounce of parental energy. Spool made me feel special. He decked me out with surveillance gadgets and a lip balm that fired laser beams. He gave me a technologically altered tracksuit and sneakers. He made me believe my biological father wanted me to apprentice in the spy world so we'd have common ground when we finally got to spend time together.

It was all a lie. Section 23 wanted Carter Strike in captivity. They used me to get to him. But together Strike and I brought Section 23 to its knees and put Spool permanently out of commission. (Ironically, I helped bring about that last bit with the laser lip balm Spool gave me.)

I hoped, now that Strike was back in my life and my family had accepted him, we'd go on more secret spy adventures, that he'd teach me everything he learned during his years in the field. But when I actually spoke the words "Teach me everything you learned during your years in the spy field," Strike's reply was "Forget any of this ever happened. Don't dwell on it. Move on. Take it from an old burned-out spy, this is not the life you want. Be normal, stay normal. That's the best advice I can give you."

That was horrible advice and the last thing I wanted to hear. But Strike thought he was doing the right thing. If I persisted in my demands, there was a chance Strike would see his presence in my life as doing more harm than good. He might disappear again, this time maybe permanently.

So I don't try to talk to him about gadgets or surveillance or double agents anymore. When I visit him in his new condo in Suntop Hills, a strip mall–dominated area a few miles from my family's house, he tries out new recipes he learned from the Food Network. Other times, we play his *PGA Tour* video game, and there are dark moments when he insists on making me suffer through this horrific old country song called "If I Could Only Win Your Love" that sounds like two geese being strangled. Sometimes we talk about school and what colleges I might want to attend and sometimes, awkwardly, boys.

But not one particular boy. Not Dale Tookey, the double agent Strike assigned to monitor me at Reindeer Crescent Middle School. The genius hacker who helped me save my little sister, Natalie, from the boss of Section 23 when he drugged and abducted her. The same Dale Tookey I kissed twice and then watched drive away (in a Smart Car programmed to talk with my voice). I don't know where he is. I don't know who he's working for. I don't know if he's still alive. Strike, who recruited and trained him, only ever answers my questions with a shrug. "Don't dwell on it," he repeats. "Move on."

It's been six months since Strike nailed the coffin lid shut on his old life and contented himself with getting to know me and making up for all the time we were denied each other. Having him around has only strengthened my relationship with my mom and dad, with my brother, Ryan, and with Natalie. I feel complete and sure of myself in a way I never did before. In time, I'll forget I was ever any kind of spy.

But not today.

Someone's trying to set me up. Trying to make me take the fall for selling cheerleading secrets. Pushing all the right buttons. I suddenly find I'm tingling with excitement. Like I'm a spy again!

# CHAPTER THREE

# Blabby

"Who do you think it is?" asks my friend Joanna. "Brendan Chew?"

Brendan Chew, my former nemesis and one-time class clown, simmers with resentment every time our paths cross. The fool who used to take huge pleasure in calling me Midget Wilder is still bitter over the definitive way I shut down his shenanigans. (Let's remember together: I pulled back an arm as if to hit him. Chew flinched. I said, "This midget just made you pee your big-boy pants." Everybody laughed. Happy memories.)

"Brendan Chew is like Tinker Bell," I tell Joanna.

"He needs the love and applause of a gullible audience. Setting me up for cheerleader-choreography theft is way too anonymous and complicated for someone like him."

"That's exactly why it might be him," she says. "You wouldn't expect it." Then she yells, "I know, I'm coming! I said I'm coming! I'll call you later, Bridget." And the phone goes dead.

Even though I still talk to Joanna Conquest on my way to and from school, as I have every day for what feels like the past fifty years, she doesn't live in Reindeer Crescent anymore. Four months ago, her grandmother, the woman she affectionately—as affectionately as Joanna is capable of—refers to as Big Log took a tumble on her way downstairs. She tripped, it turns out, on a discarded yogurt carton. A carton emblazoned with the words *Mine. Don't touch!* in Joanna's scrawl. Old bones take a while to heal and Big Log's recuperation at Reindeer Crescent Memorial Hospital turned out to be such a lengthy process that a question mark started to form over Joanna's future. She was too young to be left alone in a home filled with discarded yogurt cartons. She had no relatives in the state of California and no one to look after her.

I overheard my mom and dad having a late-night conversation about the possibility of taking her in. It was a lot like the time Dad drove over a hedgehog. They were still talking halfheartedly about bringing the wounded critter to the nearest vet when they were twenty miles away from the squished prickly mess.

The endlessly repeated joke around school was that Big Log had thrown herself downstairs rather than spend any more time around Joanna. Which was harsh but, like the meanest jokes, had the ring of truth. Joanna could be tough to take. She thought the worst of everybody, she was endlessly judgmental, and she was incapable of being happy about another person's good fortune. But when the cousins in Brooklyn she'd never mentioned saved her from getting sucked into the child services system and possibly dumped onto an unsuspecting foster family, I was surprised, pleased for her, and worried for me. I hadn't exactly told her everything about Carter Strike, Section 23, and my double life. But she'd been around for some of it. I could talk to Joanna the way I couldn't talk to anyone other than Carter Strike, and since he'd adopted the be-normal-stay-normal lifestyle, I could barely talk to him the way I talked to her.

**So, yes, I** was feeling a little abandoned when she packed up and moved three thousand miles away to New York. Joanna called me every day to keep me informed about her new home: "There's a burned-out shell of a car out front and a dead dog living inside it. That's the part they like to show visitors." She was equally enthusiastic about her new family: "Barely civilized. Like *Planet of the Apes* if the monkeys had stayed stupid." Those calls almost made up for not having her around. But then, a good spy is at her best when she's on her own with no excess baggage and no one else's feelings to consider or worry about.

By the time I get home, I have zero energy to construct credible theories as to the culprit behind my cheer-napping. I throw my backpack across the hallway and charge into the kitchen. I need a grilled cheese sandwich to refuel my throbbing, pulsing brain-thoughts. I wrench open the fridge door. And I feel an impact. There's something on the other side of the door. Something solid. I hear a faint mewl, like a cat. A cat! Has Boots followed me home? I slowly, fearfully close the fridge. I see a slight, waifish girl with a hand pressed to her forehead. Where I hit her with the door.

"Oh my God!" I gasp. "Abby. I'm so sorry. I didn't see you there. Are you okay? Is anything broken?"

Ryan's girlfriend, Abby—don't worry, we'll get to that in a moment—says something like "Mumble-mumblemumbleRyan." She says it with her tiny little mouth almost completely closed and her huge gray eyes staring over my head. Thus ends what might have been my longest conversation with Abigail Rheinhardt since Ryan brought her home from the Creepy Broken Toy Sale (or, for accuracy's sake, since she made a favorable comment about one of the prank videos on his Instagram).

I feel bad that I hit her with the fridge door but I feel worse for me because now I'm morally obligated to remain in the kitchen with Abby until Ryan shows up to take her to his room to . . . I don't know . . . feed her twigs or worms. I sound mean, don't I? Save your sympathy. For me. I'm stuck here with a fake look of concern on my face while Abby gives me nothing. Not a word. She just stands there vacantly with her arms hanging at a weird angle like they're suspended by invisible wires. I'm not even a talky-talk kind of person but she doesn't try.

It's not as if I don't have any conversational *topics* to bring up with her: You're at least sixteen but you have the affect of a nine-year-old; what's that about? That's a good one. Or how about: Why do you go out of your way to make everyone uncomfortable, and don't pretend you don't know you're doing it because you totally do? I can tell from the way you lurk around our house like you want us to think you're a ghost. But these relevant questions remain unspoken. Maybe, just maybe, there's some childhood trauma that makes Abby act the way she does. Maybe, just maybe, lurking around our house is in some way helping to heal deep wounds. And so, because I am a sensitive and caring person, I say nothing and back slowly out of the kitchen. As I leave, I hear the front door open.

"What are you doing?" yells my sister, Natalie, from behind me. "Are you hiding from Blabby?"

Natalie, still universally regarded as the nice one of the Wilder siblings, would not have used the nickname intended only as a private joke between us if she'd known Abby was standing a few feet away. But she didn't see her at first. Only I did. Only I saw the expression on Abby's face, signifying that being clobbered with the fridge door hadn't hurt her as much as discovering that we call her Blabby behind her back.

"Oh," says Natalie. She joins me in the kitchen, wearing her cheerleader uniform, and sees Abby, hands clasped, eyes downcast, toes pointed inward, a model of discomfort.

Natalie nips the flesh of my upper arm. "Did she hear me?" she whispers. "Why didn't you say something?"

The awkward moment between the three of us seems to go into slow motion. I feel like Natalie and I are frozen in time, nipping and whispering and glancing at each other as we try to not to deal with the distress we just caused Blab . . . Abby.

The awkward moment ends when Ryan shoves past us and moves toward his girlfriend. It's like watching a magnet pick up a safety pin. She enfolds herself into him like she's an extra limb growing out of his armpit. She gazes adoringly up at my brother and says something like "MumblemumblemumbleRyan."

"That car I said I was going to look at," he replies. It's almost as if he understands what she's saying. She arches up on tiptoes to kiss him. Natalie and I curl our lips and clutch our stomachs at the exact same time. This is a revolting display but somehow we can't look away. Ryan stops mid-kiss and touches a concerned finger to the fading red mark on Abby's forehead. She mumblemumbles something and he gives us a dirty look.

"Nice," he says, shaking his head to let us know we're not nice. To the untrained eye, Natalie in her Cheerminator gear and me with what I like to think is my understated coolness might seem like the mean clique of oppressors, and Abby might seem like the poor innocent outcast who got hit with a door and then insulted, but . . . actually, at this moment, it's hard to make a convincing case for me and Natalie.

"You're jerks, you know that?" says Ryan. He leaves

the kitchen with Blabby clinging to him.

As he passes me, he mutters, "You better be nicer to her. I kept your secrets."

During the time Brian Spool had me convinced I was a fully functioning spy, Ryan saw me in action. He saw me kick butt (including his) and he covered for me when I snuck out at night. There isn't much he could do with that information. Certainly nothing that could damage me. But just the fact that he knows something gives him a smidgen of power over me. I meet his eye and give him the faintest acknowledgment that I understand what he's saying.

Natalie and I wait in silence until we hear Ryan's bedroom door close.

"You called her Blabby! To her face!" I yell.

Natalie waves away my accusation. She goes to the fridge—the scene of the crime!—removes a carton of almond milk, and pours herself a glass.

"What was it, like six, eight weeks ago, every word out of his mouth was a lie? He broke stuff and stole things and stayed out all night?" I marvel. "Now: whole different Ryan."

"I liked the old one better," says Natalie, wiping her mouth. "If he has to date anyone, it shouldn't be that drip. It reflects badly on us. Doesn't someone in your class have a big sister with partial vision or a life-threatening ill-ness? Someone better than Blabby he could go out with?" Natalie leaves the kitchen. "That's a nice little project for you. I know you can handle it. Don't let me down."

"How is it my project?" I call after her. But she skips happily upstairs, leaving the Blabby Project in my hands.

So now I've got to find out who set me up to take the fall for the Cheerminator choreography scam and then I need to disentangle Ryan from Blabby.

My phone vibrates. I look at the screen. Two texts. Both from Carter Strike.

**Did your parents talk to you yet?**
**I didn't do it.**

# CHAPTER FOUR

# Strike Out

"It's nothing," says my mom.

"It's fine," says my dad.

I do not believe a word my parents are saying. They came home late. They keep shooting shifty little glances at each other. They talk louder than normal. They laugh louder and they laugh a lot. This is especially noticeable in my mom. Nancy Wilder is not what you'd call a chuckler or a chortler. She is not amused by jokes or sitcoms or YouTube clips of people walking into walls. That isn't to say she doesn't have a sense of humor. "I'm just not one of those big laughers," she has said in the past. She is tonight, though.

"Sorry I'm so late. One of those days when everything just boom-boom-boom . . . one thing after another HAHAHA!" "Your brother upstairs with whatshername? She should just move in. Maybe she already has HAHAHA!"

Mom sounds like an alien from a planet where the concept of laughter is unknown who's attempting to fit in with us Earth folk by impersonating the sounds we make when amused. Dad is also acting like an alien. An alien amazed by the long black plastic object with the buttons that makes pictures appear and disappear on the big flat screen attached to the wall. Jeff Wilder is not a channel flipper. Jeff Wilder likes to settle into his brown leather chair and watch a *Law & Order* marathon or a baseball game that goes into extra innings. Tonight, though, he's jabbing the remote at the TV screen, hurtling through channels, flying past makeover shows, renovation shows, pawnshop shows, dance studio shows, haunted house shows, and cake-baking shows.

"Dad, *Bait Car*," I say as he zips past one of our old obsessions. He keeps on flipping, but at the same time, he reaches out to the half-empty pizza box and tears off a piece of the buffalo chicken pie. Mom takes the occasional nibble of her tepid slice between bursts of forced laughter. These are the people who told me "It's nothing" and "It's fine" when I asked them if anything was wrong.

I know something is up. I knew it when Strike sent me those texts designed to send alarm bells clanging in my head. I knew it when he failed to respond to my many, many return texts, calls, and emails. I knew it when Jeff and Nancy Wilder came home from their respective jobs an hour later than usual, he from managing the local Pottery Barn, she from the courier company she runs, Wheel Getit2u.

They came home together. They came bearing pizza. And they requested the pleasure of my company. Not Ryan and Blabby, who, they claimed, they didn't want to disturb (or, more likely, be disturbed by). Not Natalie, whose Cheerminator health regime meant pizza was a no-no. So, just Bridget in the living room with her laughing mother and flipping father. Both of them chomping down morsels of pizza and looking like it was giving them as much pleasure as eating dirty concrete.

"What's wrong?" I ask. Again.

Dad looks at Mom. Mom looks at Dad. She stops laughing. He hits the Power button, turning the screen black. Dad leans forward. Mom sits down on the couch and pats the cushion next to her. They both have these half smiles and wide eyes that say, *Trust us. We love you.*

Uh-oh.

Whatever's coming, I'm not going to enjoy it.

I sit on the end of the couch, leaving two cushions between me and my non-laughing mother. I notice pink foam packing chips at her feet, the kind companies use to fill crates so that the items inside don't get damaged. The floor of my mom's workplace is ankle-deep in them. She must have tracked them into the house and not noticed, which, like the laughing, is out of character for her and evidence that something is on her mind.

"We like Carter Strike," she says.

I say nothing.

"We were surprised the way you made contact with him. We'd rather you'd talked to us first and let us approach him. But we know what it meant to you to meet your biological father and we're glad you got to know him."

She looks over at Dad. His turn.

"And we like him. He's a good guy. He's made what could have been an awkward situation comfortable for all of us. He's got your best interests at heart, I really believe that, in spite of . . ."

*Clang clang clang!*

"In spite of?" I repeat.

Dad finishes his slice. Mom sighs. Ball's back in her court.

"We're home a little bit later than usual tonight because . . . I had a kind of a crisis at work . . ."

"Boom-boom-boom. One thing after another," I say. I don't try to copy her forced laugh.

She nods. "One of our vans that should have been back in the depot never returned. You know we got that account with the software company I was telling you about?"

I pretend I do.

"This was one of our first big jobs with them. A lot of specs and samples going to clients. The driver made a couple of the deliveries on his schedule and then the van went missing."

**Did your parents talk to you yet?**

**I didn't do it.**

I feel myself flush.

Mom picks up speed. "I called the police. They found the van. It only took about . . ."

"A half hour. Forty minutes tops," says Dad. "They got on it."

"They found it in Suntop Hills," says my mom, looking straight at me. "Outside Carter Strike's condo."

"But that doesn't mean he's got anything to do with it," I say. I hear my voice echo around the living room.

"No one's saying it does," Dad assures me.

"But the van was empty," says Mom.

"There's seventeen apartments in that building," I say. "Some of them have four or five people in them." I try to do the math and figure out how many potentially guilty parties that makes. I'm no good at math.

"The police have been able to make contact with them and they've all been able to account for what they were doing. All except . . ."

**I didn't do it.**

"The police haven't been able to contact Carter," says Dad. "He's not answering his phone. If he's in his apartment, he's not opening the door." He leans forward in his chair, making a gun with his hand. "Remember that *Law & Order* episode where Briscoe decided there were exigent circumstances and he didn't need a warrant to gain access to the perp's house? That could happen here. They could just break in."

"No one's breaking in," says Mom. "We're not anywhere near the stage where anyone's considering pressing charges. I just think . . . has Carter made contact with you at any time today?"

I need to be very careful how I respond to this. If I pick a fight with my parents over their lack of faith in Strike, which I sort of want to do, it will create a situation where they feel competitive with him and they'll want to prove how responsible and protective they are. Which will result in me being watched a lot more closely. If I indulge in a hysterical foot-stamping tantrum, they'll think he's been overindulging me—maybe spoiling me with stolen gifts? I can't be seen to defend him too aggressively. All I can fall back on is the one emotion that I'm honestly feeling right at this moment: confusion.

"I don't understand," I say. "Why would he . . . I mean, he has that rug business . . . I don't understand . . . This must be a coincidence . . . Will you tell me if the police find out anything?"

Mom bridges the two-cushion gap between us and tries to my ease my distress with a soothing hug.

"Of course we will. And if Carter calls you, you'll let us know immediately?"

Dad hauls himself up from the depths of his leather chair. He sits on the arm of the couch stroking my hair.

"And maybe from now on, when you go over to his place, one of us should come with you."

*Say nothing.*

I let my legitimately concerned parents continue to hug and stroke me. Strike's innocent. I know Strike's innocent. I'm pretty sure Strike's innocent. Why would he steal software from one of my mom's vans? He wouldn't. Unless he hadn't moved on. Unless he was still knee-deep in secret spy business. Why would he send me those texts unless he knew he was going to be accused of something? Unless he really wanted me to believe he had nothing to with it.

Unless, unless, unless . . .

# CHAPTER FIVE

# *Mildly Liked*

"Really, Bridget? *Really?* How much more awesome? How much bigger and better? Do you have a chocolate fountain made of gold?"

Casey Breakbush's face is bright red, her eyes are wild, her hair is perfect. Her two constant companions, Kelly Beach and Nola Milligan, purse their lips, put their hands on their hips, and shake their heads in synchronized disapproval. Casey's face is inches from mine. I hear her breathe. She sounds like she just ran a mile. Except the energy she would have devoted to that, she's using to hate me. And I don't know why.

I've been in school approximately ninety-six seconds. I have not looked at nor spoken to anyone. My thoughts, up until this second, have been exclusively focused on the elusive Carter Strike, who, since yesterday's alarming texts, has remained off the radar.

"Why, Bridget?" Casey is revving up again. "For what? What does it get you?"

A small crowd of onlookers, including several Cheerminators, shoot suspicious glances my way, taking the temperature of this confrontation. Will it be worth filming? Will it turn physical? Will there be hair pulling and face slapping? I hope not, for Casey's sake, because Section 23 may have lied to me and manipulated me, but they also molded me into quite a tough little cookie.

Casey puts her hands together. I brace myself, ready to block a sudden slap. She starts applauding. Kelly and Nola join in. There's a smattering of applause from the onlookers.

"Great performance. Totally bought it. I trusted you. I thought we were friends."

Now I'm really confused. There was a brief moment, back when I was Brian Spool's unquestioning puppet, when I cunningly infiltrated Casey, Kelly, and Nola's airtight friendship. For a moment, I breathed the same rarefied peach-scented air as these slim, pretty girls. But they were smarter than I thought and they saw through me. They smelled a rat where Bridget Wilder was concerned. They never fully froze me out, though. They nod hello at me from time to time. But friends, Casey?

She thrusts her phone in my face. Like, right in my face. Screen against nose. The same way Big Bow Valkyrie confronted me yesterday.

I step back a few inches. The phone continues to hover close.

"What?" I finally say. "What am I supposed to be looking at?"

Kelly's applause grows more vigorous. "Stop!" she cries. "Enough! There's no more awards."

"How about a Phony?" says Nola. "Like a Tony, but for someone who's completely fake."

Not bad. I give her an impressed look and return my attention to the phone held tightly in Casey's hand. I see an Instagram party invitation. A party invitation for an awesome event three nights from now. A party that's going to be so stellar and packed with excitement and magic it will ruin the lives of anyone who does not attend. A party that will make the parties of anyone unlucky enough to be throwing similar events on the same night look shameful and embarrassing. A party thrown by . . . wait a minute . . . unless there's another Bridget

Wilder attending Reindeer Crescent Middle School, this insanely opulent and extravagant party seems like it's being thrown by me.

"But . . . I'm not having a party." I gulp. "I didn't write this."

Kelly starts applauding again.

"Stop clapping," I yell. "This wasn't me. I'm not . . ."

"Not trying to get attention by having a pathetic excuse for a party on the same night as Casey's birthday?" says Kelly.

"No!" I yelp. Oh my God, this is just like the Cheerminator accusation.

"It's fine, Bridget," says Casey, her voice suddenly calm and serene. "Have your party. I hope it's a big success. I hope it is packed with excitement and magic. But why do you have to be mean? Why would you put me down to make yourself look good?"

"But . . . but . . . but," I splutter. I hear the onlookers immediately start imitating me. Is Brendan Chew in the crowd? Yup. Camera phone capturing every second of my discomfort. Already working up his "butt butt butt" impression.

"Casey." I sort of want to take her hand to emphasize my sincerity. But I also fear she'd pull it away and demand the nurse sterilize it.

"Casey," I say again. "I'm not having a party. I've never had a party. I probably will never have a party."

"You're having a pity party right now," smirks Nola. Zing.

I ignore her and stay focused on Casey. "And even if, for some reason, I was having a party, why would I for a second consider having it on the same night as yours? Think about it. For one, I would be spending the weeks running up to your birthday hoping that maybe I'd get an invitation."

"Don't hold your breath. Or do," sneers Nola.

"Two. I'm mildly liked."

Casey stares at me, unsure of what I just said.

"You don't throw a party, especially not one with that kind of hype, if you're only mildly liked. You're either a total mystery and are going all out to make a name for yourself or you're deluded about your level of popularity. I'm neither of these things. Some people think I'm okay. Some people find me sort of annoying. Nobody has strong feelings about me either way. I'm mildly liked."

Casey blinks a few times and jiggles her phone at me. "You didn't do this?"

"Do you really think I did? I mean, really?"

"Then who?" says Casey. She turns to Kelly and Nola. They walk away, deep in fast, whispery, paranoid conversation. I am forgotten.

Except by the person who's having fun messing with me. Who has the time and malice to weasel their way into my Instagram account? Who wants to see me in a constant state of squirming embarrassment? I glance at the onlookers as they melt away. One of you, perhaps? I watch Brendan Chew mouthing "butt butt butt" to a grinning fellow student. You?

If only I had my Glasses of Truth rather than my normal Glasses of Vision, or my Tic Tac cameras, or my beloved laser lip balm, but Section 23 confiscated most of the gadgets that made me such a powerhouse spy. Am I capable of hunting down my clever tormentor armed with just the power of my own instincts? Maybe. But right now I feel a little bit fragile. That mildly liked thing struck too close to home. (Would it hurt Dale Tookey to send me a single text?) I bet Strike has a souvenir or two from his days as a Section 23 agent. I bet he's got a little stock of gadgets hidden away in that condo of his.

I decide that's as good an excuse as any to head out to Suntop Hills and pay my biological father, the retired spy, a visit.

# CHAPTER SIX

# The Virus Club

The inside of Strike's apartment looks like the aftermath of a crime. A few white cardboard containers from a local Chinese restaurant sit on top of his coffee table, along with three remote controls and a few discarded pages from the sports section of an old copy of the *LA Times*. A vinyl turntable, the most expensive item in the room, is plugged into the wall beside Strike's deep, saggy leather couch. A small pile of ancient 45s and albums nests on the floor, along with a big pair of headphones. I take a quick look at the single on the turntable. My heart sinks. "If I Could Only Win Your Love" by the Strangled Geese—again!

I texted my mom that I was going to the debut meeting of the Virus Club, an after-school group dedicated to studying and talking about the spread of rare and deadly diseases around the world. She texted me back one word: ugh. It was a bizarre lie designed to buy me a couple of hours before my presence would be missed at home. But as I pad slowly through Strike's living room to the small kitchen, it occurs to me I wasn't lying. I really am attending a meeting of the Virus Club. Dishes are piled up in the sink. Grease stains mark the white stove top. More Chinese food containers and a half-full peanut butter jar are the only occupants of the fridge. I back out of the kitchen and head toward the bathroom. Towels are strewn on the floor and there's a constant *drip-drip-drip* from the shower. Empty shampoo bottles lie by the side of the trash can below the sink, almost as if someone threw them from the shower when they were done and never bothered picking them up. I pause outside Strike's bedroom door. This is a clear invasion of his privacy. Yes, he gave me a key and told me to drop by anytime, but I'm starting to feel like an intruder.

"Strike," I call out. "It's me. Bridget. Wilder." Should I remind him how we're related? I grit my teeth and push open the door to his inner sanctum.

Well, there's the rest of the *LA Times*, some of it spread across his California King–size bed, some of it on the floor with footprints smudging the ink. Four pillows are stacked up against the headboard, allowing him to watch the big-screen TV that hasn't been attached to the wall but is perched on top of an old trunk. No pictures anywhere. No framed photos. No posters. No signs of life. In fact, the entire apartment looks exactly like it has on the other occasions I've been here.

"This place isn't fit for pigs," I told him on each of my last few visits.

"Next time you come it will be," he kept promising. "I'm cleaning it all up. Top to bottom."

Maybe I should take on that mammoth task while I'm here. Find a bucket and mop and surprise him with a fresh, clean, uncluttered apartment when he comes home. If he ever comes home.

I hear a sound outside the front door. The sound of a key entering a lock. I sag with relief. Strike's back. I don't have to clean his smelly house! I hurry out of the bedroom. As I move into the living room, I can hear that the key being pushed into the lock doesn't fit. I go to open the door. Then I stop. A different key is being pushed hard into the door. With similar lack of success. I freeze. A third key opens the door.

I turn and run.

Someone's in the house. My instinct tells me it's not Strike. I pull off my sneakers in case they slap against the floorboards and give me away. I need a hiding place. The bathroom? Like Mom said: ugh. I make my way back into Strike's bedroom, close the door behind me as quietly as I can, and then look for somewhere I won't be found. I squat down and peer under Strike's bed. There might be space for me to hide but I am not lying under there. I can see things growing!

I also notice a small, octagonal-shaped piece of black plastic no bigger than a quarter. Perhaps a discarded gadget from Strike's Section 23 days? I'm tempted to risk touching the forest of mold to grab it but I hear the footsteps getting closer.

I slide open the closet, pull the door closed after me, and squeeze past the rails of shirts and jackets. There's more room than I thought back here. Not only that, it's cleaner and neater than the rest of Strike's apartment. A few wooden file cabinets are pushed against the sides and a safe is built into the wall. On impulse, I open one of the cabinet drawers. Empty. I try a few others. Nothing there. I tiptoe over to the safe. As I get closer, I see scratches and dents surrounding the steel lock. Someone's already tried to gain access.

I stare at the lock. Anagrams are my thing, not combinations of numbers. I have no hope of opening this safe, yet I suddenly find that I very much want to open it because A) it's there and B) others before me have tried and failed.

I reach out for the lock and give it a quick, exploratory twist. It's cold to the touch and hard to budge. I twist a little more. With an effort that causes a sharp pain to shoot up my arm, I get the lock to move. The sequence of numbers I try might seem a bit self-centered, but Strike moved to this smelly condo to be near me. He put himself in harm's way to save me on more than one occasion. Why wouldn't the combination to his wall safe be my birth date? 8242002. I turn the lock until the sequence is complete. On the final 2, the door opens.

I feel a quick burst of emotions. I'm obviously enormously proud of myself for solving a numbers-based problem. I feel incredibly touched that Strike would choose my birth date. I hadn't recognized how close a relationship we've developed in such a short time and now I'm scared. Scared that I don't know where he is. Or what sort of trouble he's in.

I reach inside the open door and pull out a box. A rectangular metal box. Light, silver-colored. Something small, round, and loose rolls around inside.

"Give it to me," says a low, muffled voice.

I gasp in shock. I'm not saying I'd forgotten why I was hiding back here, but I'd hoped I was safely hidden. The intruder follows my path past Strike's shirts and jackets. I can't see his face. It's completely covered by an eyeless black mask.

But I can see the gun. The one he's pointing straight at my face.

# CHAPTER SEVEN

# Balls of Fury

"Is Strike okay?" I ask the masked intruder in as non-quavery a voice as I can muster. "What did you do to him?"

In reply, the man goes to grab the metal box from my grasp. I let go before he takes hold. The box falls on the ground and the lid bursts open. Round glass multicolored balls roll chaotically across the ground.

"Marbles?" I say. "Who keeps marbles in a safe?"

I drop to my knees to pick them up. I hear a grunt and look up to see the black eyeless mask gazing down in my direction. How does he see? He grabs me roughly by the elbow and jerks me upright. I am not going to give him the satisfaction of showing fear or displaying any sign he's caused me pain. He pushes the gun close to my face. I don't know how good a job I'm doing of hiding my fear.

From behind me, I hear a weird rumbling sound like a train passing underneath.

Down on the floor, the marbles that fell out of the tin have formed a straight line and are rolling toward us seemingly under their own power. The marble at the head of the line suddenly hurtles into the air and flies— literally flies—down the barrel of Black Mask's gun.

The noise from under his mask is a mixture of shock and anger. He shakes the gun to remove the marble. There are no circumstances in which I want to be around an angry black-masked man furiously shaking a gun. But I really don't want to be around such a guy when he's shaking his gun in a small hidden compartment in the back of a closet. I start to sneak past him, but he bars my way with his free arm.

That's when I see the marbles fly up his sleeve. I think there's about twenty of them, but it's easy to lose count because they're moving so fast and they're mar-bles! His arm is jerked up in the air and then backward. I hear a crack and a muffled howl from beneath the mask. He drops his gun and tries to pull off his jacket. I watch in fascination as more marbles swarm up the legs of his pants. Suddenly, he's a kicking, stamping, flailing explosion of uncontrollable limbs. He can't reestablish dominance of his arms or his legs. The marbles walk him backward out of the closet. All the while, increasingly hysterical muffled screams come from under the mask. I think I see something move under there. Something small and round. A few somethings that are small and round. And then the screaming stops.

Black Mask staggers backward. He makes a valiant attempt to claw the mask off his face, but whatever's in his sleeves makes his arms flap like a demented bird. He loses his balance and falls backward. He lands with a thud on the ground. But he doesn't lie there. He's slowly rolled away.

I have not moved for the past couple of minutes. I don't know if I've even breathed. I just stand in Strike's closet and stare, not quite able to process what I just saw.

And then the marbles come back.

They're rolling in a circular formation now. Picking up speed, making a sort of *rrrrrr* sound as they rumble toward me. I squeeze my eyes shut and hug myself, fearing what happened to Black Mask is now going to happen to me.

I hear the marbles *rrrrrr* straight past me. I open a

cautious eye. I glance down at the ground. One by one, the marbles hop back into the metal box. When the last one is safe inside, the lid snaps shut.

**"Nanomarbles," I explain** to Black Mask as he returns to consciousness. He says something like "Mmm mmmm mmmm." After he's come to terms with the fact that his mouth has been sealed with an extra-strong, extra-sticky brand of duct tape from Strike's laughable excuse for a supply closet, he starts to struggle. And then he realizes his wrists and ankles have been similarly bound to the rickety wooden chair on which he sits in the living room. He gives me a look of pure loathing. It doesn't fit the somewhat angelic face I saw when I peeled off the scary rubber mask. He looks more like he should be singing in a church choir, except for those eyes, which are boring straight into me and wishing me a life of pain and misery.

I jiggle the silver metal box at him. His eyes widen. His "mmmm mmmm"'s have a hint of panic.

"I used to have a black-and-gold tracksuit that was nanopowered. So I like to think I'm up to speed with the latest in nanotechnology. That's why I think these little critters . . ."

Once again, I shake the box, and this time close to his face so he hears the glass inhabitants clatter off one another. He flinches and rears back, almost falling off the chair.

". . . are nanopowered. If I let them loose, they'd probably find some new parts of you to explore. Or we could just talk."

Still holding the box, I move carefully to the back of the wooden chair. I take hold of the end of the tape, and with one not-quite-as-smooth-as-I'd-hoped pull, it rips away from his mouth.

"Aaaaah!" is the first thing he says. I wince at the red marks on his lip and chin.

"Where's Strike?" I demand.

In reply, he eases back in the chair, tilts his head, and gives me a cold look through half-closed eyes.

"Who are you?" I say.

Again, nothing.

"Who do you work for? Section 23?"

I harbor a secret fear that, even though I ended Brian Spool, his organization might have regrouped like a worm that grows a new head after the old is cut off.

Non-Black Mask gives me a pitying look and a smirk. So the good news is, he doesn't work for Section 23. The bad news is, his smug expression suggests whoever he does work for makes Section 23 look like a lemonade stand.

His smile and his continued silence chip away at my confidence, as, I'm sure, was his intent. I could let the nanomarbles loose on him again, but I have no idea how to control them. They may leave him incapable of giving me any information about Strike.

I put the metal marble box on the coffee table, walk to the side of the saggy couch, and pick up Strike's big headphones. I place them over Non-Black Mask's ears. Then I switch on the turntable and put the needle on the 45. The sound that has marred many a visit to Suntop Hills fills the intruder's ears. I watch him squirm as the nasal, yodelly vocals begin. As soon as he sees the amused look on my face, he starts nodding along, acting like he enjoys the whining in his ears. Let's see how he likes it the next twenty-seven times I make him endure it.

As the awful song plays, I walk around the living room letting Non-Black Mask see how little his presence interests me. I stop a few feet away from the front door. There's something on the floor. A few flattened objects, some green, some white. I reach cautiously down to pick one up. It's a foam packing chip. My mom's been here!

Or . . . Non-Black Mask must have unknowingly tracked them in. That seems the more likely option. But what would he have been packing? I slip a couple of the foam chips into my pocket. The song on the turntable reaches its whiny conclusion and I make my way over and restart it. The superior look on his face is gone, replaced by a rebellious one. *I can wait this out*, it says.

We'll see.

I walk back into Strike's bedroom. Holding my breath, I crouch down and look under his bed. Still hideous and unhygienic. I reach for the small, black, octagonal object. At first I think it might be an abandoned piece of chocolate and, for about an eighth of a second, consider putting in my mouth. I shudder and return to my senses. It seems to be plastic. It feels hard, it has the thickness of a coin, and it's grooved around the edges. If it's not a Section 23 gadget, maybe I can pretend it is and use it to intimidate Non-Black Mask. I slip it in my pocket and return to the living room, where, once again, my favorite song is coming to a close.

He wears his defiant expression as I take up position in front of him. I reach in my pocket and pull out the foam packing chips.

"What was in the crate?"

He tilts his head toward the turntable, daring me to play it again. This strategy might not have worked the way I hoped it would. I want to hear this stupid song less than he does and I can only hear the tinny sound that spills through the headphones.

I pull the little black octagon from my pocket and place it in the palm of my hand. I hold it out to him.

Everything changes.

His eyes widen. He struggles with the duct tape that binds him and tries to push the wooden chair away from me.

"Don't . . ." He's actually speaking! Why didn't I do this right away instead of making myself suffer through that stupid song again? "Be careful with that. Put it down," he says, trying to sound calm and failing. Good gadget instinct, Bridget!

"Why?" I ask. "What does it do? What happens if I do . . . this?"

I pretend to throw it at him. He lets out a noise that sounds like *yeep*.

I watch his panicked eyes flutter around the room. They fall on his mask, which I suddenly suspect he wasn't wearing just to be scary. He was wearing it because he didn't want to breathe in anything toxic.

I walk across the living room, pick up his black mask, and put it over my face. The smell of dried sweat and rubber is not fragrant. The mask may be featureless to the terrified observer, but on the inside, there are small breathing holes dotted around the nose and mouth areas. It's like looking through a thin curtain. I can see enough to know the guy in the chair is currently very nervous and fidgety. I get close to him so he can understand my muffled voice. I hold up the little black octagon.

"I don't know what this does. But I'm guessing what I'm wearing means it doesn't affect me."

I flip the chip in the air and catch it.

"It's not a toy," he screeches.

"Okay. Now we're getting somewhere. You're finally giving me a little information. Keep going."

I flip the octagon again.

"Stop! You'll set it off. It triggers a powerful sedative."

I pull off the mask. Too smelly.

"What was it doing under Strike's bed? Why are there foam packing chips on the ground? Did you sedate Strike so you could pack him in a crate and send him somewhere?"

The guy grimaces at my questions. I push the octagon closer to his face. He sighs and gives me a nod.

"He's going to be fine. If he cooperates."

"Cooperates with who?" I shout at him. "Who's got him? Why would they need to sedate him?"

"You need to walk away now," the guy shouts back, and I suddenly see emotion in his face. "Don't get involved in this. It's too big for you. Go now and I won't tell anyone you were here."

"I'm not going anywhere," I snap. "You packed my

biological father in a crate like he's a . . . a . . . hat stand. Or something. Tell me where he is!"

I stare at him. He stares back.

I feel a sudden, insistent tapping at my foot. I look down. A little red marble is bouncing off the side of my shoe. I reach down to pick it up. It hops up and down in my palm.

"No, don't . . . ," says the guy in the chair.

"I'm not—" is all I manage to get out.

The red marble bounces from my palm inside the guy's jacket. He squirms and moans in fear and discomfort. I hear the sound of glass clinking against plastic.

My phone receives a text.

I inhale sharply. My first thought is, *Mom!* She's found out there is no Virus Club.

But a quick look at my phone tells a different story. A much nuttier story. A text has been forwarded from another phone. Presumably, the guy in the chair's phone.

**Crate leaving Farmer's Field Arr NYC: 7AM**

The red marble hops out of the guy's jacket—where it had been searching his phone!—and back into my hand. I look down at the glass ball.

"Thanks, Red," I say. The marble bounces up and down in my palm and then jumps into my pocket. Strike may be unconscious inside a packing crate in a plane bound for New York, but at least I've made a new friend.

"So we've got the where," I tell the guy. "Now we need the why. Are you recruiting him, is that it?"

The guy almost smiles. "That broken-down old has-been? We just need him for . . ."

"Leverage?" One of Brian Spool's favorite words. One I hoped I'd never hear again. "What leverage does having Strike in a crate get you?"

He shakes his head. "I gave you a chance," he says. "I told you to leave. That's all you get from me."

I see from the resolve in his face that he's not kidding. I could play the awful song again. I could let Red and his/her friends take a crack at him. But I've been here too long. I check my watch. It's after six. I need to go home and figure out what to do with the little information I have.

I toss the guy his mask. It lands in his lap. He starts to struggle and pull against the tape.

I go to leave Strike's apartment. As I do, I drop the octagonal device on the ground and stamp down hard on it.

The guy yells, "Nooooo!"

I'm out the door a second later. Behind me, I leave only silence.

# CHAPTER EIGHT

# Frequent Liar

A glass ball has thus far proven more resourceful than me at locating Strike's current location. I'm tempted to let my new friend Red figure out my next move. Maybe the smart nanomarble knows a way to stop the plane before it takes off and spring Strike from the crate where he currently slumbers. What would Dale Tookey do? I wonder. I'm no genius hacker, obviously, but if I put myself in the mind of a two- or three-year-old Tookey, maybe I can answer some basic questions. How do I find out where Strike's crate is leaving from? Where is it headed? What happens to the crate after the plane touches down?

On the bus home from Strike's condo, I pull out my phone and make the following discoveries:

Farmer's Field is a private airport on the southeast side of Sacramento.

If I Google the words *flight tracker*, I find many sites devoted to recording every aircraft, no matter how tiny, that takes off from any airport, no matter how tiny, anywhere in the world.

It will not be hard for me to keep tabs on the flight taking Strike and his crate to New York City.

There is a geo-fencing app that allows the user to set up boundaries around a particular location. Whenever a person, vehicle, animal, or crate bearing a comatose biological father leaves the geo-fenced boundaries, the geo-fencer—i.e., me—gets a text and an email with a satellite view.

In theory, I will be able to track any movement to and from the plane carrying Strike.

If I Google the words *live traffic cam*, I find many sites devoted to showing footage of dirty, rain-soaked highways with vehicles thundering past.

In theory, I will be able to keep continuous eyes on whatever is being used to transport Strike. The investigation into who set me up with the cheerleaders and the birthday invite will have to wait.

By the time I get home, I am not exactly confident I'm

as technologically adept as a two-year-old Dale Tookey, or even a red marble. But at least I have a plan. Or at least part of a plan. As I walk in the door, I prepare myself to put the other part into operation.

"How was Virus Club?" Dad calls out.

"Are they naming one after you?" Ryan. Of course. "One that crawls under your skin and irritates you more the longer it hangs around?"

I ignore my brother, who sits on the top of the stairs. Then I mosey into the kitchen, where Dad is annihilating an avocado. Already annihilated bits of sautéed chicken are piled up on a plate next to him. He's making guacamole tacos. I have approximately five minutes before he goes into a taco-eating coma and everything not taco-related becomes a blur to him.

"Tacos on the way," he says, mid-avocado destruction. "Hope you're hungry."

I go to the fridge and bring out a container of pomegranates and a lime.

"You're reading my mind," he says.

I roll the lime on the kitchen worktop and slice it in half.

"I talked to Joanna before," I say as I cut the lime.

"Who?" he says. "Oh, yeah. Of course. How's she doing in . . . um . . . Phila . . . Pittsbur . . . Brooklyn?"

"Not great," I say. "She's finding it hard to fit in."

"Hard to imagine why," says Ryan, who has snuck into the kitchen. He grabs a lime half and goes to squirt it in my face.

"Not smart when I'm holding a knife," I snarl.

"Cut it out, you two," says Dad.

"You two?" I repeat, outraged. "I could have lost an eye!"

Ryan takes a suck of the lime and screws up his face. "Look," he says, "it's almost like having Joanna right here in the kitchen."

He's hugely not funny but I'm grateful for the opportunity to get back on message.

"Joanna doesn't make friends easily. Her relatives . . . I mean, it was amazing of them to take her in, but . . ."

"Your mother and I seriously considered it," says Dad. His blatant bald-faced lie makes me feel less guilty about what I'm building up to say.

"I'd love to go and see her," I say, like I haven't been working out the exact right way to phrase this request so it doesn't sound desperate or suspicious. "Just, you know, spend a couple of days hanging out. Let her know she's still got a friend."

"That's the most beautiful, selfless thing I've ever heard," sobs Ryan. He squeezes little droplets of lime juice under his eyes to let me know how touched he is by my idea.

Suddenly, he lets out a loud yelp of pain and clutches his neck. As he does, I feel a movement inside my jacket pocket. As if something just jumped out and then bounced back in. Thank you, Red!

Ryan shoots me a furious look. Like he wants to pin the out-of-nowhere assault on me but can't quite figure out a way to do it.

"When would you want to go?" Dad says.

"Right now," says Ryan. "I'll help her pack."

"You really want to be away from home over Thanksgiving or Christmas?"

"Take the whole of winter," says Ryan.

I put a preemptive hand in my pocket and clutch the restless Red.

"Columbus Day's coming up," I say. Like I haven't thought about it. "I could go for the weekend. I'd be in constant touch. Ten texts a minute and pictures, endless pictures and clips of me at Yankee Stadium."

Dad keeps pummeling avocado. I glance at Ryan. He wants this just as much as me.

"Let me run this crazy idea by your mother," Dad says. He pulls out his phone and one-finger types a text to Mom. I mentally compile alternative scenarios if Mom no-nos the Joanna visit scam. Maybe Sacramento

Regional Transit has randomly selected me to ride the New York City subway system and then share my findings on the viability of a local subway system? Kind of far-fetched, I agree. Dad's text message effect tinkles. He looks at his screen and then at me.

"We've got air miles piled up we've never used. I think we've got enough for you . . ."

"Thankyouthankyouthankyou," I gasp. I rush to hug him but stop short. We both have knives in our hands.

". . . and Ryan to go for the weekend," he says.

I put the knife down. Just in case.

"What?" I say

"What?" Ryan repeats.

"He can be your—" Dad starts.

"I'm closer to fourteen than thirteen. I don't need a chaperone," I shout. "Babies, actual babies, travel on planes by themselves. I don't need someone, especially him, coming along with me . . ."

I made expansive calculations as to how I was going to swing this trip to New York to save Strike. I did not foresee getting permission so easily but I also did not foresee this bombshell. How can I do my spy business with Ryan tagging along squirting lime juice in my eye?

I'm aware the louder I get and the more I glare at my father, the more I'm liable to put my spontaneous trip in jeopardy. I try to calm down. As I do, I suddenly hear from behind me, "MumblemumblemumbleRyan."

Great. Blabby has manifested from the ether. I don't even need to turn around to see her wrapping herself around Ryan. But I do and she is.

My brother grins at me. "Abby has family in NYC. They'd be happy to send her a ticket so she could come and double-chaperone you."

"Double what?" I bawl.

"You're going to be falling down holes and choking on hot dogs. You need eyes on you at all times," he says.

Abby buries herself deep inside Ryan's elbow. He gives me a smirk of triumph. I rein in my distaste and shrug in return. Will I enjoy traveling with them? I'd rather spend time sleeping under Strike's bed, but the grim presence of Blabby removes the potential annoyance of having Ryan get in my way once I begin my mission. He'll be so entangled in her web—I'm not being fanciful, she has little tendrils of spider web hanging off her hair and her clothing—he won't notice me.

I thank Dad with a peck on the cheek. Then I charge upstairs to nail down my travel plans for the next few days.

CHAPTER NINE

# The Welcoming Committee

"Bridget, Abby needs to sit next to the window or she gets anxious."

"Bridget, get up and let Abby pass, she needs to go to the bathroom."

"Bridget, Abby doesn't want her pasta. You take it and give her your chicken."

"Bridget, you don't need your pillow. Abby can't get comfortable unless she has two."

This early morning flight from Sacramento International Airport to JFK in New York is the worst journey anyone has ever endured. Not only did the person seated in front of me shove their chair back as far as it was capable of going, leaving me approximately no space whatsoever, not only is the person behind me so entertained by whatever they're watching on their seat-back screen that they're moved to kick my chair every seven seconds, not only am I denied any escape from this nightmare because my—and only my—seat-back screen is not functioning and, despite my mentioning this on two occasions to Kimber the flight attendant, nothing has been done to fix it. Not only do I have to suffer all these indignities, but I'm stranded on a plane for six hours with Abby.

Subtract the time she spends mumblemumble-mumbling to Ryan. And the time they spend touching their noses together and darting squelchy little kisses at each other. And the time she slumps unconscious against the window with her tiny mouth hanging open. And the time she crawls around in her seat trying to get comfortable. And the time she spends complaining to Ryan that she can't get comfortable even with my pillow! And that's still an unreasonable amount of time for anyone to have to spend eighteen inches away from Abby, her anxieties, her allergies, and her abnormally tiny bladder.

In between changing seats for Abby, changing my meal for Abby, and getting up to let Abby scamper off to the bathroom seventeen times an hour, I spend the rest of the pleasant voyage buried in my laptop. Before Dad drove us to the airport early this morning—fun fact: Abby gets carsick in the front *and* back seat!—my attempts to track Strike's plane proved successful. The single-engine jet vehicle landed at Teterboro Airport in New Jersey. Ten minutes after the plane landed, a van exited the air-field. Through the wonders of the geo-fencing app, I am able to get a satellite picture of the van, and with the help of various live traffic cams, I have been able to follow it during the flight. The van takes the Holland Tunnel to New York. It makes various lefts and rights before turning onto Broadway.

Maybe Strike's in a show? Maybe sedating him and flying him in a crate is a way to combat his stage fright? Probably not.

Next time I check, the van has come to what seems to be the end of its journey. It stops outside something called the Dominion Brothers Building. A quick search reveals the following facts: The building dates back to 1913. It was named after the two brothers who sank their discount retail store fortunes into it. Frustrated by the cheapskate reputation their stores gave them, the brothers designed the building to be an awe-inspiring testament to their expensive taste. The reception area was built to look like a cathedral with a vast domed ceiling and sweeping marble staircases. The building was, briefly, the tallest construction in New York. Unfortunately, the asking price for the apartments and office spaces in the building was so astronomic, more than half of the available floors remained uninhabited. The current asking price is $110 million. Guided tours around the ground floor continue on an hourly basis. I am about to read more when Ryan taps my arm.

"Bridget, get up and let Abby pass . . ."

I can't believe this. I have to put my tray table up, close my laptop, undo my seat belt, and wriggle out of my seat again? Can't she hold it? Apparently she can't. Before I can even push my tray table back in position, she's up and squeezing past Ryan. Suddenly, she lurches toward me, knocking Ryan's half-finished can of soda from its precarious perch on the arm of his seat. The contents foam all over my jeans and seep into the keyboard of my laptop.

"Mumblemumblemumbleturbulence," I think I hear her say as she regains her balance and pushes past me.

I stare after her in disbelief. I turn to Ryan and wordlessly invite him to join me in staring after her in disbelief.

"*Always in the Way: My Story by Bridget Wilder,*" he says.

I say nothing. But inside I'm boiling with rage and I'm thinking, *That's not my story. I have an epic story.* And buried deep inside there will be a footnote that will say, *There was no turbulence. She did that on purpose and she will pay.*

**I part ways** with Ryan and Blabby at the baggage carousel in JFK. Ryan and I make plans to check in with each other every few hours so our stories are straight when Mom and Dad call. We plan to meet on Monday at lunchtime so we can travel back to the airport together and catch our afternoon flight home.

"You going to be all right by yourself? You don't want me to wait with you till Happy Face gets here?" says Ryan, showing a tiny amount of brotherly concern for the first time this trip.

I shake my head no. "I'm fine. Go do your thing." I don't even want to imagine what Ryan and Blabby's thing might be.

Ryan hovers for a second. Surely there isn't a hug coming? He settles on giving me a fleeting squeeze on the upper arm. And then he's gone, teetering under the weight of his overnight case and Blabby's bag of billowing nightgowns for unwell Victorian children. (I'm guessing that's what's in there. It could be the remains of an actual Victorian child.)

As for me, I'm traveling light. My backpack contains a few changes of clothes, a toothbrush, my soda-drenched laptop, a few mini Snickers bars, and a box of marbles. It hits me that I'm venturing into unknown territory comparatively gadget-free, at least compared to the version of me that opened Brian Spool's Pandora's box of gadgets and could run like the wind, detect a lie from the merest twitch, and laser-beam a car in two.

Now it's just me and marbles. The marbles, I know, have the element of surprise on their side. They're a lot more aggressive than I am and they show no fear going places I would never venture. But are we enough? Yes, we subdued an intruder; yes, we found our target; yes, we lied our way across the country, but now what? Black Mask was one guy. One guy who wasn't expecting me or marbles. Whoever he works for knows about us now. Whoever he works for has the resources to put Carter Strike in a crate and fly him in a private plane across the country. I feel the confidence that got me to the baggage carousel start to dribble away. I'm on my own in a big strange city.

Fighting the urge to get back on the plane, I trudge toward the arrivals gate, where happy families are being reunited with loved ones. And how do I treat my own family? I lie my face off to them so I can save a guy I play a golf video game with every few weeks. I see more weary passengers light up as they spot their loved ones smiling and waving at them. One particular family smiles, waves, and beckons in my direction. I keep trudging toward the exit.

"Bridget!" a few voices yell.

The smiling, waving, beckoning family is smiling, waving, and beckoning at me! And now that I focus on them, I see a very familiar face, although not a face I have ever previously associated with smiling.

When I contacted Joanna about my sudden East Coast trip, I was straight with her that I needed an alibi. This wasn't a hang out and catch up visit, this was me doing something mysterious connected to my enigmatic other life. And yet, here's Joanna, meeting me at the airport with . . . let's see who we've got here: a woman in her late thirties with lots of curly brown hair, several elaborately knotted scarves, and glasses pushed up on her forehead; a young boy, maybe five or six, clinging to Joanna's leg, who she's not kicking away or trying to stomp. And then there's a tall skinny boy, maybe my age, maybe a little older, with a shaved head, gray hoodie, and a Stop Bullying Now T-shirt. He seems just as enthused by my presence as the rest of the group Joanna described as barely civilized apes.

"Sam, please help Bridget with her bag," says the scarf-laden woman as I approach them.

The boy with the shaved head eagerly goes to take my carry-on.

"I'm good," I tell this Sam person with a grateful smile. I don't want a stranger anywhere near the marbles.

"I didn't mean to express male privilege," he says, looking concerned.

"Alex Gunnery," says the woman, sweeping me up into a vanilla-scented embrace. The feel of her scarves against my face is like a cool breeze on a summer day.

"Lovely to meet you," she says in a rich, velvety voice. "Jojo told us so much about you. Finally we get to meet the famous Bridget Wilder."

"Jojo's been telling me all about *you*," I reply in as rainbow-filled a manner as I can manage while simultaneously shooting Joanna a look that says, *What part of alibi did you fail to understand?*

"Did she tell you I've been to the moon?" says the little tyke, smiling to show the gap where his two front teeth should be.

"That's our secret, Lucien," Joanna says, and she puts her hand on his head and ruffles his hair!

The only reason the Joanna I know would do such a thing would be to rub chewing gum into the boy's hair. But this is not the Joanna I know. This is someone I don't recognize, whose actions are incomprehensible to me, who seems . . . happy?

*"Avanti!"* Alex Gunnery suddenly sings out. "Lots of ground to cover. Lots of stops to make. You're going to see a whole different side of Brooklyn, Bridget!"

"That's great," I chirp back.

The lovely Mrs. Gunnery heads out of the airport. Her tribe follows. I grab Joanna's arm and pull her back.

"Why the welcoming committee? Why am I going to see a whole different side of Brooklyn?"

Joanna shifts from foot to foot. She seems to not want to meet my gaze.

"I don't know," she mutters. "They're clingy. I think they've put hidden cameras in my room. Something weird is going on with them."

As she says this, Joanna turns away from me and looks longingly at the departing Gunnery family as if a second away from their presence is depriving her of oxygen.

Like I thought . . . she's happy!

"Joanna," I say. "Did you want me to meet them because you really like them?"

She flushes bright red. "Are you demented? No, I don't like them. I just . . . I couldn't get rid of them. You know, like you used to have lice you couldn't get rid of."

I feel a warm glow of familiarity as the Joanna I know makes a belated reappearance.

"I'm glad you've found a home where you're happy," I say. "And you and that little moon kid are adorable together, but the fewer people who know I'm here, the better."

"That's what I told them," says Joanna. "But they made up this whole stupid list of things they wanted to do with you. Flea markets and thrift stores and little coffee shops where there's this kind of freestyle poetry reading and anyone can get up to read."

Joanna's not just smiling when she tells me this; she has a wistful look on her face I've never seen before.

"I mean, I hate it," she says quickly. "The words don't even rhyme."

I'm in something of a predicament here. Strike is my reason for lying my way across the country, but my grumpy best friend is unexpectedly happy and, even though it would physically pain her to admit it, wants me to share in her happiness. The least I can do is spend a little family time with Joanna and the lovely Gunnerys, even if it's only so I can cynically use them to help me accomplish my spy mission.

# CHAPTER TEN

# Modern Family

I'm in the back of Alex Gunnery's SUV as it makes its stop-and-start-journey along the dull, gray expressway to Brooklyn. Our drive back from the airport is taking so long, Mrs. Gunnery informs us, because the eldest son of a high-ranking official from the government of someplace called Trezekhastan is celebrating his fourteenth birthday tomorrow and half of Trezekhastan is making its way into New York to join in the festivities.

"Trezekhastani children undergo such a fascinating rite of passage," says Mrs. Gunnery. "It's my understanding they have a service where they bid farewell to all their favorite childhood keepsakes, whether they be toys or bicycles or books. It's hard to imagine a tradition like that catching on in America, right, guys? We love our possessions too much."

"I don't know," Sam replies. "Material things don't matter as much as the strong bonds of family and friendship."

I laugh out loud at this parent-pleasing nonsense, but as I do, I realize I am the only one laughing and I quickly turn my laugh into a racking cough. (It goes something like "Ha-ha-ha-hacccchhhh-haaaaccchhh.")

"That sounds nasty, Bridget," says Alex.

"I'm fine," I assure her.

"Sam," she says, "remind me to make Bridget a jug of my therapeutic licorice-root tea when we get home."

Sam dutifully inputs the instruction into his phone.

Little Lucien sits next to me, playing rock-paper-scissors with Joanna. Again, adorable. (Especially when he says *thissers* because of his missing front teeth.) Sam is up front, shooting periodic glances at his phone but mostly listening to and agreeing with his mother, who is now yammering about the Brooklyn Flea. For a second, I thought she was painting a cautionary picture of a winged predator found only in her community. But now that I pay a little more attention, she is talking at great length about the exciting flea market where she works most weekends selling antique furniture and overpriced trinkets.

"Jojo's been a big help at the stall," pipes up Sam. "She's a real people person."

I am so glad not to be drinking Alex's licorice-root tea at the moment Sam says this or liquid would be spraying out of my nose. I give Joanna a sidelong glance of amazement but she does not divert her attention from little Lucien.

"You'll get to see her in action on Saturday," promises Mrs. Gunnery. "And that's not the only treat I've got lined up for you." She grins at Sam. "Should I tell her?"

"Why not?" smiles Sam.

Mrs. Gunnery gives a little shiver of anticipation. She checks to see that the traffic ahead is moving slowly enough to look back at me without causing a horrific accident, then she squeezes around and says, "I'm taking you to Nasturtium!"

"Really?" breathes Joanna, like she's just heard she's been nominated the new pope. "It's back?"

Mrs. Gunnery turns to give the busy road ahead her undivided attention, but that doesn't mean she stops talking. The words come pouring out of her. Nasturtium is the most amazing pop-up vegan restaurant anyone has ever been to ever. The meal they served her earlier this year changed her life. Literally.

"Mine too," says Sam, who seems like every parent's dream child.

"Remember the saffron coconut curry with rainbow cauliflower and cilantro pesto, Jojo?" says Mrs. Gunnery. "A religious experience." She lets out a loud groan. "You're in for a rare treat, Bridget. Something to tell the folks back home."

Forget for a second that I'm Bridget Wilder: Spy. Focus instead on the fact that I'm Bridget Wilder of the Sacramento Wilders. My dad makes guacamole tacos—and not the healthy kind! We eat at Leatherby's Family Creamery. We shared a buffalo chicken pizza just the other night. I beat up my school's Big Green healthy eating vending machine. I like food that tastes good. This fancy-pants vegan stuff is not for me. And it's certainly not for Joanna, who I've seen snap into a Slim Jim on numerous occasions. If I were legitimately in New York to visit with my best friend, I'd be freaking out over the way she's swapped her true—i.e., unpleasant—personality to fit in with her warm, caring, and slightly irritating relatives.

If I had time, I would take Joanna by the shoulders and shake some sense into her. "Remember who you are," I'd bark. "Remember the Conquest Report? All that bitterness and spite: Was it for nothing?" But I don't have time. I have a missing father to find.

"Uh, Mrs. Gunnery?" I say.

"Alex, please."

"Alex. This sounds like an amazing weekend. It's so thoughtful of you to have planned out my whole visit."

"It's my absolute pleasure, Bridget," she says.

"There's something else I'd like to do while I'm here."

Alex frowns a little at this. *Control freak*, I think, pleased to see even a slight flaw in her motherly perfection.

"There's this place in Manhattan. I'm sure you know it. The Dominion Brothers Building? On Broadway? I've always wanted to see it. Me and Jojo both."

Joanna gives me a sharp look. I raise my eyebrows at her. *Have my back here.*

"Right" is as much as she's prepared to mumble.

Not me. I'm in full-on lie mode. My plan is to hide in plain sight among a bustling tribe of Gunnerys while I scope out the building and look for clues pointing to Strike's whereabouts. So I put on a hushed, breathless voice and let the dishonesty flood out: "The ambition of those brothers. The sense of history in that building. It's so inspiring to me. I just . . . I don't know, this probably sounds stupid . . ."

"Don't undermine yourself like that, Bridget," says Alex. "Go on."

"We're all listening," adds Sam, needlessly.

"I always thought, and I know I'm speaking for Joanna as well, that I'd be just as inspired if I was ever lucky enough to be able to . . ."

*Screeeech.*

Alex drags the SUV across two lanes of traffic, amid horn honking and fist shaking from angry drivers. She takes the exit to Manhattan. As she drives toward the city, she launches into a story about the buildings, churches, and libraries that inspired her when she was even younger than me. I make the occasional *ooh* or *wow* sound but I'm not really listening to a word she says. Carter Strike may have wanted me to be-normal-stay-normal, but the spy in me cannot be denied. I made it across the country more or less under my own steam. I was able to track down the location of my abducted biological father. And now I'm going to blend into the bosom of this warm, caring, annoying, and entirely unsuspecting family. Until it's time to go into spy mode.

# CHAPTER ELEVEN

# Bleak House

Gargoyles with leather wings, horned heads, clawed hands, and bared fangs grimace down from the concrete tower at the top of the Dominion Brothers Building.

"There's your boyfriend," says Joanna, pointing upward. This sudden flash of the real Joanna startles me and also gives me a pang of sorrow about the continued absence of Dale Tookey from my life. Not that he was ever my boyfriend, obviously.

"Good call, B," says Alex Gunnery, gazing up at the full dark majesty of the building. "I've worked in the city for years but I don't know it, not the way I should. I must have walked past this magnificent, imposing structure a hundred times and been so wrapped up in my little world that I didn't even notice the grandeur that was right under my nose. And then you come in from"—she wrinkles her nose in distaste—"California. From the suburbs. And it's you who teaches me to open my eyes." She throws an arm over my shoulder and draws me in close to her. The fall wind blows those billowing scarves into my face. Alex looks up at the Dominion Brothers Building and lets out a long sigh. I don't want to seem rude so I refrain from pulling away, but I find myself wondering what lies behind those windows. Is Carter Strike in one of those rooms? Is he still sedated, still packed inside a wooden crate with no idea of his location? Is he being tortured in there? Is he even still alive?

I let out a sudden, involuntary moan of fear.

"I know, B," says Alex, pulling me all the way into her arms and embracing me until I'm fully consumed inside the masses of scarves. "We're just so small and insignificant. But art gives our lives meaning. It makes us immortal."

I disentangle myself from Alex and point to the arched entrance to the building.

"We should head inside," I say.

*"Avanti,"* she agrees, probably not meaning to be irritating.

**I may have** pretended to be awestruck by the very idea of visiting the Dominion Brothers Building but now that I'm in the actual lobby, there's no pretense. My eyes are bugging out and my jaw is on the floor (not literally. That would require medical attention). Little Lucien is running around with his arms spread open and his head thrown back, gazing up at the twinkling, glass-mosaic domed ceiling hundreds of feet above us. He's screaming "Waaaaaaah!" I know what he means. Everything in the lobby is oversize and spectacular. Huge concrete pillars surround us. The staircases, although roped off to the public, are as sweeping and spectacular as advertised. Beneath our feet, the vast black floor tiles are embedded with what I'm guessing are actual diamonds. Portraits of the Dominion Brothers carved in stone look down on us from the cornices.

"Six days after the building to which he'd devoted his every waking hour was finally unveiled, Arthur Dominion jumped from the twenty-second floor," says a tour guide to the small, stunned gaggle of tourists following in his wake.

"Did he die?" asks one tourist.

"He did not survive," says the guide. "But some say his ghostly presence still roams the tower of the building."

"Waaaaaah!" screams little Lucien as he runs toward the tourists, arms flailing.

Some of the out-of-towners gasp in fear, as if Lucien is possessed by the spirit of Arthur Dominion. Joanna runs after Lucien to restrain him but he thinks she's playing a fun game with him, which only amps him up to new heights of running and shrieking. Two uniformed security guards emerge from behind the pillars and head straight for Joanna and Lucien. Alex, who up to this minute has been lost in the sheer opulence of the lobby, snaps out of her reverie and hurries to calm her child. All of this is pretty much what I hoped would happen when I secretly slipped little Lucien a mini Snickers as his mom parked the SUV.

With the guards, the lobby staff, and the tourists' attention all directed toward the sugar-crazed Lucien, I am free to do a quick sweep of my surroundings. There is a visitors' desk where guests sign in, and the official in charge of the desk sits facing a computer screen that offers surveillance feeds taken from cameras all over the building. I need to see those feeds. I need to see if there's footage of Strike. I need to know if his crate was delivered to this address and I need to find out who received the delivery. At the front of the visitors' desk is a panel containing a list of all the occupants rich enough to live or work in the Dominion Brothers Building. I see names of real estate tycoons. I see banks from all over the world. I see the American Hook and Tin Company on the thirty-ninth floor. But I do not see anything above that. After all these years, half of the building remains empty.

Feigning interest in the diamond-studded floor tiles, I make my way toward a bank of six golden elevator doors. Two men and a woman wait for the elevators to descend. All three wear business suits. All three have important airs about them, as if they're powerful people with much to accomplish and little time to do it. None of the three acknowledge one another. One of the gold doors slides open. The two men hang back. The woman enters. A second elevator door opens. One of the two men walks inside. A third door opens. The last of the three disappears through the doors.

I watch the gold clocks above each door showing the ascension of the elevators. The first one stops at the thirty-ninth floor. So does the second. I look at the third gold clock. Once again, the journey ends at the thirty-ninth floor. My spy senses tingle. Three people who traveled to the same destination but did not ride together. Maybe each of them felt too important to mix with the others?

Maybe there's bad blood between the hook people and the tin people? Maybe getting off on the same floor was just an incredible coincidence? Maybe not.

I glance around the lobby. Little Lucien is still flailing around. Joanna is still trying to catch him. Alex is deep in conversation with the security guards. She's making big extravagant hand gestures and the guards look like they want to retreat behind the pillars. I make my way back to the elevators. When the first gold door opens, I hop inside. The walls, floor, and ceiling of the elevator are mirrored. I see a million plucky young spies trying to look like we're ready for anything. I press gold button number thirty-nine. Nothing happens. The doors remain open. I try again.

"You need one of these," says Sam Gunnery, standing in front of me holding up a white plastic key card, and grinning as if to let me know that he knows something about me. Something secret.

# CHAPTER TWELVE

# Son of a Gunnery

"The cards are embedded with a code that changes on a daily basis," says Sam Gunnery. "So they don't fall into the wrong hands."

The Sam Gunnery facing me between the gold elevator doors is not the same slightly sappy, eager-to-please, perfect son who feared I might have been offended by his offer to carry my backpack. He's not the same boy who hung on his mother's every word in the SUV. He's a different guy. I don't know much about him, but I do know one thing. He's waiting for me to say "So how did you get one?"

He looks in the mirror behind me.

"Security," he says.

I look over his shoulder. There's a guard approaching.

He steps inside and swipes the card across a scanner above the gold number buttons. The doors slide shut. He does not press another button. We're not moving. There is silence in the elevator between me, this version of Sam Gunnery, and our million reflections.

"I knew," he says. "I knew from your face when you saw us all at JFK. I knew when you started in on Alex about your lifelong obsession with the Dominion Brothers Building. I knew when you sent the *frère* into sugar shock. You're not here to hang out with Jojo. You're here for something else. Something that involves this," he says, holding the key card close to my face and then pulling it away.

"You don't know anything," I say. I don't like what's happening here. I don't like the way he's talking to me. I don't like that he made me think he was one thing and now he turns out to be quite another. And obviously I don't like that he has something I want. Most of all, I don't like that I am now forced to gesture to the plastic key card in his hand and utter the words, "So how did you get one?"

He raises a finger in the air, takes out his phone, scrolls through a few texts, and then sends a couple of replies. I have no doubt he is doing this to demonstrate that he currently has the upper hand. Now, I don't think he does have the upper hand. I think my spy background gives me the way upper hand. But that self-same spy training reminds me that the Sam Gunnery pretending to be engrossed in his phone is not the sappy Sam Gunnery I thought I knew. So in fact, right now neither of us has the upper hand. I wait patiently for him to slip his phone back into his pocket.

He gives me an *oh, you're still here?* smirk. Holding the key card between forefinger and thumb, he says, "Someone did me a favor because I did them a favor. And now I'm in a position to do you a favor, which I really want to do. But first I need to know what you can do for me."

I feel like applauding Sam Gunnery the way Casey, Kelly, and Nola applauded me when they believed I was feigning innocence over the whole rival party thing. Except Sam Gunnery is really good. The guy his family believes him to be and the cocky, cool, calculating hustler wondering how best to exploit me are two radically different humans.

I could just kick the card out of his hand. I have a really good, really fast kick. But we're in an enclosed space. Shattering a mirror or damaging the elevator might trigger a hundred alarms. I have a better idea.

"Here's what I can do for you," I say.

I take Red out of my pocket and let him see it in my open palm.

"Is that a marble?" he says.

"A red one." I nod.

"Is it your special one?" he asks, in a tone that suggests he thinks he's talking to a small child.

"Yes, it is," I say.

I open my palm and Red shoots across the elevator and drops into the pocket where Sam keeps his phone.

This is how cocky, cool, and calculating Sam Gunnery appears to be. I won't say his eyes don't widen. I won't say he doesn't flinch as Red makes contact with his cell phone. But he doesn't freak out the way I hoped he would.

Red jumps back into my hand.

My phone announces a text has arrived. I remove it from my pocket.

"Okay, how did you . . . what is that . . . where did you get it?" Finally, I get the flustered reaction I was waiting for.

I raise a finger in the air, leisurely look at my phone, scroll through a few texts, and then I look up at him with what I hope is an infuriatingly smug *oh, you're still here?* smirk.

"Gg45 wants a plus-one for the secret Action Bronson show, cheetamode has a source for the green camo Pumas you wanted, and tedb says, Where's the money you owe me, I ain't asking again . . ."

"Okay, stop," says Sam. "What do you need from me that will get me one of whatever that thing is?"

"I need access to the building's surveillance camera feeds—from first thing this morning till now."

Sam takes out his phone and sends a text. He looks up at me. "That all?"

"Seriously?" I say. "It's done?"

"Good as," he says. "The Squirrel's on it."

Sam correctly interprets my reaction as dubious.

"This squirelly little hacker who's hugely in my debt. He needed a place to hide out for reasons I don't need to know. I hooked him up, so he'll get right on it. What's next on the list?"

This Sam Gunnery seems very full of himself, but I could use a thimbleful of his confidence right now when I'm in a strange town and wildly out of my depth on a mission I've barely prepared for

"Thirty-ninth floor," I say.

He presses the gold button. The elevator starts to rise.

"Alex," he says into his phone, "Bridget Wilder and I are going to hang out here a while. There's an archive section with some of the original blueprints. The history of this place is so rich and inspiring, I really feel like I'm learning to see through the architect's eyes. Why don't you and the kids head home? I'll introduce Bridget to the wonders of the Brooklyn-bound F train and we'll catch up with you later. Good idea? Love you lots."

He smiles at me. "That's how it's done."

"How what's done?" I say. "Why the torrent of lies? You're not coming with me."

"Listen, Bridget Wilder, if that's even your name, you and your marble owe me. You're not going anywhere till that little red thing is in my hand."

I'm about to protest, but the truth is, Sam Gunnery appears to be a very, very connected guy and, even by my own lofty standards, a very, very skilled liar. He also seems to have a whole lot of experience keeping secrets, so why wouldn't I want him around as I blunder into unknown territory?

"Fine," I pretend to sulk as we rise past the four-teenth floor. "Say nothing, ask no questions, don't get in my way. Do your best to be unobtrusive, check in with your squirrel about my surveillance feeds, and then you'll get a marble."

"A *marble*?" he says. "I want that marble." He points at Red.

"Really?" I say, in a tone that suggests I'm talking to a small child. "You like the bright shiny color? You don't think that might be the prototype and I've got access to a more advanced model?"

"Um . . ." is all he can manage. The truth is, I like Red's bright shiny color; I like the way he—I've decided he's a he—nestles in my palm. I feel an emotional attachment to the little fellow. Maybe I'm not a cat person after all. (Sorry, Boots.) I'm not giving Red to Sam Gunnery. I'll give him a different marble from the metal box. I'm pretty sure it'll bounce up his nose and then come rolling back to me.

The elevator passes the high twenties. Sam starts sniffing the air close to my face. I back away from him.

"Don't get weird around me, Gunnery," I warn. "Or no marble for you."

"Just thought I picked up a familiar scent," he says, smirk in place. "The smell of looming disappointment. I know how this is going to turn out. You're stalking your favorite boy band member. Or some guy you've been following on Instagram. That's where this is going."

I know what he's doing. He's trying to goad me into telling him why I'm in an elevator in New York with a box full of nanomarbles. Information is power for guys like him. The thing is, I want to tell him. We're both liars, we both lead double lives. Why not share?

"What did Joanna tell you about me?" I ask.

He has to think about it. "Your sister's really popular." He nibbles on his lower lip. "You play the clarinet?"

"That's it?" I squeak. "And it's the flute. I play the flute."

"I'm sure you're very talented," he says, amused by my outrage.

"Not as a flautist," I say. "But I do have other skills."

He says nothing. I opened this door. Am I reckless enough to charge through it? I gesture to him to move closer to me. He inches forward. I lower my voice, letting him know what I'm about to tell him is classified information.

"My dad—my biological one, not the one who's raised me—is a spy. Was a spy."

This isn't going as smoothly as I'd hoped. Do I stop now or keep stumbling along? I opt to stumble.

"The people he worked for trained me to be a secret agent, except it was a setup so they could smoke my father out of hiding. But I turned it around on them and I cut a Mercedes in half with a laser-powered lip balm and put them out of business. But now he—my biological dad—has been kidnapped. Someone put him in a crate and shipped him here to New York. I don't know exactly where but I think he's in this building and I have to find him before something bad happens to him. So. When's that squirrel of yours going to find those camera feeds?"

Wow. My face got really red during that recap of my interesting life. Sam Gunnery's expression is impossible to read. He doesn't look amused or dubious or horrified. He retains his cocky, cool, calculating veneer.

"At least you have some idea where your dad is," he says, and just for a second, I get a glimpse of a Sam Gunnery who isn't an eager-to-please mother's boy or a cocky, cool calculator.

Then the elevator reaches the thirty-ninth floor. The doors hiss open to reveal Carter Strike.

"Small world," he says.

# CHAPTER THIRTEEN

# Strike Back

A wave of shock crashes over me. Then a wave of relief. Then a wave of affection. Then a wave of anger. That's a lot of waves. I run out of the elevator and throw my arms around Strike. I pull away and punch him on the arm.

"Ow!" he says.

"I was scared to death. You send me those texts and then you vanish. You could have been dead!"

He gestures to himself. "Not dead," he says. I notice he's lost a little weight. The being-packed-in-a-crate diet has its advantages.

"But I'd never have known," I say, my voice shaking. "I had to find you. I had to go to your reeking apartment and overpower an intruder. I had to learn how to geofence. It's really hard! I had to lie to my family and my friend. I was worried I'd never see you again."

"But you tracked me down," says Strike, with a hint of pride.

His eyebrows raise as he notices Sam Gunnery. "And you brought a friend."

"You don't look like a spy" are Gunnery's first words to Strike. I watch Strike's face harden and I wince. Why did I think trusting some kid I just met with my secrets was such an awesome idea?

"He's not really a friend," I say quickly. "And he was just leaving."

"He doesn't have to," says Strike to Gunnery. "Any friend of Bridget's."

"Again, not a friend," I say. I shove Strike away from the elevator door, and as I do, I whisper, "Don't you think we need to talk? That guy in your apartment? The crate? The empty van outside your house? This place? What's going on?"

Strike puts his hands on my shoulders. Has he gotten taller? I check to see if he's wearing platform shoes.

"I know you've got a lot of questions. I understand

these last few days have been stressful for you. I wish you hadn't had to go through all that, but there's something I need you to see."

Strike sounds calm. Not like a guy who's been stuck in a crate for ten hours. I feel like a rookie for panicking. This is Carter Strike. He's been in far more hazardous situations. That crate was probably like a hotel room to him. He probably passed the time formulating a strategy to turn the situation to his advantage. If he's here in New York, it's because he wants to be. The half smile on his face and his total lack of freak-outedness causes me to relax and shed my worries.

He throws an arm over my shoulder and holds out his other hand to Gunnery.

"Where are my manners?" he says. "Carter Strike."

Gunnery says his name and tries to fake Strike out with a multileveled hip-hop handshake ending in an explode. This kid is so annoying! Strike matches him level for level. Gunnery looks deflated but also impressed. I direct a quick, disapproving headshake his way.

"Attempt to be cool, Gunnery," I mutter.

"Let's go, guys," says Strike.

In the middle of the thirty-ninth floor is an unmarked steel door with a security keypad on the upper right-hand side.

"This is the American Hook and Tin Company?" I say.

Strike presses six digits. The door unlocks. He pulls it open and ushers us inside.

I see no hooks or tin. What I see is a vast and never-ending library, but it's not the like the Reindeer Crescent school library. It's more like the Reindeer Crescent school football field. The bookshelves are around eight feet high and surround the entire floor. Wheeled wooden ladders provide access to the top shelves. I count thirty reading tables, each with six chairs, spaced in rows of five. The shelves and the floors are the same shade of dark brown burnished wood. I'm stunned by the size and unexpectedness of it. I want to see Gunnery's reaction, but he's staring at his phone. I give up on Gunnery and look at Strike. He smiles and points a finger upward.

There are ten stories above the thirty-ninth floor, and from where I stand I can see past floors of glass-paneled offices all the way up to the domed rooftop, where a series of interlocking skylights form the shape of a huge D for Dominion.

I exhale and turn to Strike, who nods and says, "I know."

"So what is this place?" I say. "It's not the American Hook and Tin Company. It's a cover, right?"

Gunnery touches my arm. I wave him away. This is important. I turn back to Strike.

"For what? What's really going on up here? Why is it hidden away? How come there's no floor listed above thirty-nine?"

Gunnery taps me on the wrist. "Wilder," he says.

"Not now," I snap. I focus on Strike.

"I was wrong to worry about you but you were even wronger for letting me worry. You should have let me know you were okay. We're in each other's lives now."

"You're right," Strike says. "I'm selfish and thoughtless. Old habits die hard. But now that you're here . . ."

"Wilder," says Gunnery, gripping my hand and actually dragging me away from Strike.

I whirl on him. "What?" Would anyone really blame me for giving this kid a good hard kick on the side of the head?

"The Squirrel delivered," he says, and holds up his phone for me to see.

His screen shows the feed taken from a surveillance camera. There are two figures on the screen. Their movements are jerky and the feed freezes every few seconds, but I can make out two men running through a parking garage. The man being pursued is Carter Strike.

"Tell the Squirrel he's a little bit late," I say.

"Check the time code," says Gunnery.

On the top left corner of the screen, the time reads 15:15:09.

I look at my watch. It's fifteen minutes after three.

"You guys hungry?" says Strike.

I stare at my biological father. He seemed taller. He seemed thinner. But that doesn't mean . . .

"There's an awesome cafeteria on forty-five," he says. "Best noodles in the city."

"You ever been to Yun Nan Flavor Garden?" says Gunnery.

"In Borough Park?" says Strike. "Too chewy."

"The access code you used to open the door," I say. "Is it the same combination of numbers that opens the safe in your closet?"

Strike rubs his throat. He gives me an impatient glance. "Enough talking. Let's eat."

"You can change the code after you tell me," I say. "But you're not selfish and thoughtless. You picked my birthday, right?"

He throws up his hands. "Fine. I picked your birthday."

"262003," I say.

"That's it, tell the world," says Strike.

"That's not my birthday," I say. "And you're not Carter Strike."

# CHAPTER FOURTEEN

# *Face Off*

"**Y**ou're scared, you're confused, you're tired, and you're hungry," says the man with Carter Strike's face. "You don't know what you're saying. Come upstairs and lie down. There's a quiet room on forty-six where no one will disturb you." He goes to take my arm. I jerk it away and jab my finger at him.

"Who are you?"

"Bridget, please," says the man.

I feel a violent pull behind me. It's not Gunnery, who is frozen in place looking between his phone and the man with Strike's face and back. There is something going on in my backpack. It feels like there's an animal trapped in there, trying to scratch, squirm, and kick its way free. But I don't have an animal in my backpack. I have something much more dangerous.

The man with Strike's face sighs and pulls a syringe from inside his jacket.

"I didn't want to do it this way," he says. "I wanted us to get to know each other. I wanted you to trust me."

The flap of my backpack tears open and all the marbles from my metal box shoot into the air and form a circle that revolves above the man's head.

"Backup. Now," he says, touching a hand to his ear.

The marbles above his head spin faster. I see him look up, and as he does, something happens to his face.

It's like when the picture on a TV screen starts to break up during satellite interference. His eyes and nose freeze. Then they vanish. The mouth moves but no sounds emerge. And now it's gone. The face that was there a second ago is now a hail of static. The man raises a hand to his neck. He pushes a finger under his chin and his whole face peels off.

A white face-shaped piece of plastic drops to the floor.

"His face fell off," says Gunnery.

"There's another one underneath," I say.

"He's two-faced," snorts Gunnery, who clearly loves getting the last word.

The man under what I'm guessing was some kind

of nanomask has a sallow complexion and big bulging eyes. He opens his mouth to speak, but before a word emerges, the marbles engulf him. They swarm over his face, covering his eyes, his nose, and his mouth. He tries to scream for help but the scream is muffled. He tries to tear them off but the more effort he puts out, the harder they cling. As he struggles, I see his Strike-like wig come unglued and flop onto the ground.

"Wilder!" shouts Gunnery. "The shelves!"

Gunnery points at the row of bookshelves on the far end of the library. The books disappear as a hidden door slides open. A group of black-clad, grim-faced individuals come running out. Two guys, one girl.

"Gunnery," I yell. "Take Red, find Strike!"

"Huh?" he replies.

I toss him my marble.

Gunnery catches Red and stares at him with awe. The woman who came from the shelves runs toward Gunnery. Red jumps out of his palm and rolls under the woman's left foot. She screams as her feet leave the ground and her head hits the hardwood floor with a thud that echoes around the library.

Red bounces back into Gunnery's hand.

"Follow the feed. Red'll know what to do," I yell. "Now run!"

"This is so awesome." Gunnery laughs and runs for the front door.

"I'll be fine, thanks for asking," I call after him.

Two guys, probably angry, head in my direction.

"Anytime you're ready, marbles," I call out.

They remove themselves from the face of the man who wasn't Strike and roll toward me. I feel myself rising into the air. Not high. Just about a third of an inch. Just enough for the marbles to mold themselves to the soles of my sneakers.

The fastest, angriest, and baldest of the black-clad, grim-faced backup guys reaches out to grab me. I go flying backward.

Remember the glory days of a few months ago when I was the proud owner of nanosneakers that gave me the speed and agility of a young gazelle? Those days are back!

The nanomarbles on my soles are every bit as fast as my supercharged sneakers once were. And they have to be, because my enemies are not playing.

"Don't kill her," barks the guy. "Wound her if necessary."

"I think it's going to be necessary," says the other backup guy with a Southern drawl.

The Southern guy aims something that looks like a modified Taser at me. I think back fondly to my much-missed laser lip balm with the Taser setting that I never mastered. I wish I had it now.

The Southern guy charges past his buddy and bears down on me.

"Take the shot!" yells the guy.

The Southern backup man smiles. "I believe I will." He fires. The marbles jerk me sideways and into the air. I land on the middle rung of the nearest library ladder. I kick the protruding spine of a dictionary. The ladder shoots along the shelves, whizzing me level with the Southern guy. He aims his Taser at me. I grab a book from the shelves—an encyclopedia, big and thick. The Taser darts hit the book and I let out a loud yelping laugh.

"I love a good book!" I shout.

I kick my way up the shelves, picking up speed until I see another ladder dead ahead. I tense for a head-on collision. But the marbles are ahead of me. Before the two library ladders meet in an explosion of wood and wheels, I am thrown from my rung across the library and onto the nearest reading table.

I hear a noise above me. Up on the fortieth floor, another black-clad figure is perched on top of a glass panel, aiming another weapon at me, this one a long white cylinder. To my left, the backup man leaps athletically from table to table until he's only two tables from reaching me.

"Okay, marbles, let's move," I say.

But I don't move. I stay rooted to the spot, caught between the assailant above and the guy to my left.

I try to jump out of harm's way, but the marbles will not let me move.

"Not a good time to power down," I yell.

The guy jumps toward me, his huge sinewy arms outstretched, his teeth bared. I glance up. The guy on the fortieth floor fires his weapon.

As a tiny black ball shoots straight at me, I feel a rocket launch under my feet. The marbles blast me into the air. I sail over the grasping arms of the guy. The black ball flies past me, and as it flies, it expands. The ball opens out, getting bigger and wider until I realize it has become a wire net. The net engulfs the guy, wrapping around him and then contracting, shrinking until the wire digs into his flesh, holding him tight and giving him no room to move. The bald guy falls onto the table and tries to rip his way out of the net. The more he struggles, the tighter the wires get.

I'm still being propelled into the air. The fortieth floor approaches. A few feet above me, the guy with the netgun trains his weapon on me, ready to take a second shot. I feel my right leg suddenly jerked above me. The marbles cause me to kick high and hard enough to knock the netgun out of its owner's hands. The weapon falls toward me. I grab it and fire at him. A new net blasts out of the gun and wraps around the guy on the fortieth floor. I hear him scream. I out-scream him because suddenly I'm falling.

I feel the air rush past me as I plummet back down toward the reading table. From the corner of my eye, I see the Southern guy running toward me, his Taser aimed in my direction. I tense myself for the shock of the electrodes hitting me and also for the pain of hitting the table. This is not a fun situation, but somehow I summon the presence of mind to fire the netgun at the Southern guy. The third net bursts out of the weapon just as the marbles whip me away from the table and hurl me across the library. I land gracefully on top of another table. As my marbled soles roll me to safety, I gaze at my handiwork. One backup woman groans on the ground, unable to get to her feet. The man who used to wear Strike's face lies unconscious a few feet away. The guy wrapped in netting is struggling and cursing. And the Southern guy's in a similar situation. These battle-hardened pros were tough, experienced, and armed to the teeth. And yet . . . I win!

I extend my arms and, frustrated young ballerina that I am, do a little pirouette around the reading table. (You celebrate crushing your enemies your way, I'll celebrate it mine.) My next step is to reunite with what I hope is the real Carter Strike and then get him away from this massive building and its many mysteries. I feel totally up to the task.

I roll backward off the desk, land on the ground, and let myself keep rolling for a few feet, my eyes still trained on my groaning, struggling victims.

That's what happens when you underestimate the Young Gazelle.

I feel very pleased with myself. Behind me, I hear a *sssh* sound. I turn to see a library bookshelf disappear and the elevator it was hiding open to reveal four more black-clad bad guys. Three more *sssh* sounds. Three more bookshelves vanish. I do a quick count and there are now sixteen people of various genders, ages, and sizes, armed to the teeth with guns, knives, baseball bats, lead pipes, and in one case a little ax, charging across the library floor, headed straight toward me.

It took all I had to put three bad guys out of action. How am I going to cope with sixteen?

I jump on the nearest table. The marbles break away from the soles of my sneakers and form a protective circle around me. Nice try, guys, but I have a bad feeling we're all outnumbered.

I hear a sound, kind of a splat, but quieter. Maybe a plop. Something either splatted or plopped on to the ground close to me. I search the glass-strewn floor of the gym and see something small, pink and squishy. Is that . . . gum? Semi-chewed gum?

# CHAPTER FIFTEEN

# *Gum Control*

I hear another sound. Something whooshing through the air. I look up and scream. A baseball bat is hurtling headfirst at me. The bat slams into the table, handle pointing up, and it doesn't move.

I feel the wind of an object flying over my head. A knife buries itself blade first in the table, next to the baseball bat. The knife vibrates but doesn't fall. I hear voices raised in anger. I turn to see the sixteen bad guys struggling to hold on to their weapons. There goes the little ax.

I look down at the circle of vibrating weapons that

are standing upright on the table and forming a second circle around me. Then I look at the little pink piece of half-chewed gum.

Here's a crazy thought: Is that piece of gum maybe a very powerful magnet disguised as a foodstuff? Gum is considered a foodstuff, isn't it?

"We don't need weapons," snarls a particularly angry bad guy. "Take her down."

I bend down to grab the little ax. (Is Little Ax a better nickname than the Young Gazelle?) Despite exerting a huge effort, I cannot move it. The sound of bad-guy feet against library floor becomes thunderous. I keep tugging at the little ax. It still refuses to move.

The nearest bad guy jumps toward the table.

A steel arrow shoots into the middle of the library floor. A taut wire is attached. The wire cuts the bad guy off mid-leap. He bounces against it and is thrown backward, smashing into two of his buddies, and then he crashes back down onto the ground. His head snaps to the left and he falls silent.

Three of the bad guys simply turn around and go running back to the elevators.

I smile at their sudden fear and then something touches me and I'm the scared one.

"Help!" I implore the marbles, but to no avail.

I am lifted off the ground and whisked through the

air. Invisible hands deposit me by the library ladder. I climb halfway up and watch as two more bad guys have their heads bashed together and their fists are used to punch each other in the face. The last man standing sees his moaning, twitching, broken buddies littering the gym floor. He looks up and says one word.

"Irina?"

Then his head jerks backward, and he says nothing else.

The library is suddenly silent. Except for the sound of footsteps. High heels on a wooden floor. Getting louder as they come closer to me. I don't see the person making the sound. I just hear the footsteps.

Okay, now I'm really scared.

The air in front of me begins to ripple. It forms into a translucent shape. I think it's the shape of a woman. The woman's features begin to suddenly appear, as if an artist is hastily drawing them. Her skin is pure white; her eyes are ringed with smudgy black makeup. Her hair is long and inky black. She looks like she might be in her midthirties, which, to my mind, is probably time to give up the goth look. Completing the all-black outfit favored by the occupants of this awful building is a black leather jacket zipped up to the throat. She's slightly out of breath and raises a leather-gloved hand to pat her hair back ito place. She reaches her other hand inside her jacket and pulls out something that looks like an eyedropper, a small glass pipe with a rubber squeezer at the top.

"Invisibility liquid," she says in a husky voice that has the trace of an Eastern European accent. "Not good for that to get in the wrong hands." She drops the glass pipe on the ground and stamps on it.

She holds up her palms to me. "The wrong hands." She smiles.

I don't know what to say. I remain standing halfway up the ladder. The woman comes to a halt a few feet away from me. She says nothing. I say nothing. She chews on her lower lip.

"I don't . . . ," I start to say.

"How is . . . ," she says at the exact same time.

We both stop.

"You go," she says, her big dark eyes trained on me, waiting to hear what I'm going to say.

My mind is blank. I don't know what's happening here.

My phone rings. It's probably not the best time for me to take a call, but I need a distraction.

"Mom," I say into the phone.

"Yes," says the woman.

# CHAPTER SIXTEEN

# How I Met My Mother

"Did you pack your scarf?" I hear my mom say. "It's going to be cold over the weekend. Keep your neck covered up, I don't want you coming home riddled with disease."

"I will," I say, my eyes on the pale woman standing watching me as I hang by a hand from the ladder.

"Make sure you buy Joanna's aunt a present to say thank you for letting you stay," says Mom. "Don't spend a lot of money. Just something that says we did a good job raising a polite young citizen."

"I will," I repeat.

The woman in black retreats from me and busies herself inspecting the pile of moaning, twitching bodies she demolished during the few minutes she turned invisible.

"How's Joanna coping? Does she miss the sunshine? Tell her we're all thinking about her."

"I will," I say as I watch the woman remove phones, keys, and hidden weapons from the fallen mob.

"The house is so quiet," Mom says. "Natalie's always up in her room sticking needles into voodoo dolls of the Bronze Canyon Valkyries because they beat the Cheer-minators to the Cheer Classic final thing. Your father's working his way through three seasons of that zombie show I can't watch. I miss you and your brother. Do you really have to stay the whole weekend? Can't you jump on the next plane and come home now?"

"I will," I say. The woman walks slowly away from her victims.

"Okay, you're just humoring me now. Go. Have fun. Don't break anything."

"I will," I say again as the call ends.

The woman makes her way back toward me. I continue hanging off the ladder with one hand.

"She must be worried," says the woman. "Her little girl alone in a big, strange city. I'd be worried. You're too young. I'd make you stay home."

"Luckily, it's not up to you," I say.

"We should go," she says, and holds out a hand to me. I remain hanging on the rung.

"You can ask me anything you want," she says. "I'll tell you everything. But not here. It's not safe."

"I can take care of myself," I say. I'm aware I'm being cold and unpleasant but it's the only way I can cope with this situation. I don't know this woman, I don't trust her, and I don't like the way she's acting caring and protective around me. For a young person, I have amassed a wealth of experience in being lied to and manipulated. What if this woman with the Eastern European accent is another Xan, sent to sweet-talk me into blind obedience?

"I'm well aware," says the woman. "I saw you at work in the library."

She launches into a ridiculous and inaccurate impression of my reading table pirouette of triumph. "I danced, too, as a child," she says, and gives me this big meaningful panda-eyed gaze like I'm going to throw myself into her arms.

"And I heard about Section 23, and what you did with Spool's Mercedes," she says, her bright smile revealing uneven teeth.

"How long have you been watching me?" I say, as icily as I can manage.

She tucks her hands under her elbows and looks down. Her hair falls over her face so I can't see her eyes.

"Not long," she mumbles. "There were years I tried not to think about you at all. I told myself it was better if I forgot you, but then . . ." Her voice cracks on the last word. All I see is this curtain of inky black hair covering her face. Is she making a play for my sympathy or is this what's been hiding in the back of my head since the second I heard her voice?

"Who do you work for?" I snap.

The woman sweeps her hair away from her face. "The Forties," she says.

"What's the Forties?"

"The floors of the Dominion Brothers Building from forty to forty-nine."

"The ones that were too expensive to rent out," I say, remembering the painstaking research I undertook before Blabby caused a tsunami of soda to engulf my laptop.

The woman nods. "Edward Dominion, the grandson of the brother who didn't jump out the window, found a use for them. He filled them with professionals and hired them out to the highest bidder."

"What sorts of professionals?" I ask.

The woman starts counting on her fingers. "Hackers, gangsters, leakers, con artists, kidnappers, bank robbers, blackmailers, home invaders, hired muscle, and assassins."

"Which one are you?" I ask.

The woman raises a hand for silence. I hear the elevator, the dark silent one, and start to climb.

"You want to meet my colleagues or you want to live to see your fourteenth birthday?"

"What was my birth date?" I ask.

"Twenty-fourth of August, 2002," she says. "The worst storm in twenty years. Hailstones the size of human heads."

That's easy information to access. Anyone could find that out. But just like I instinctively knew the man with Carter Strike's face was a liar, I instinctively know this woman with the pale face is not. And that means . . .

I jump down from the ladder.

The woman is unzipping her leather jacket. She reaches up behind her back and pulls a gun from a shoulder holster and a metal rod from inside her jacket pocket. She unfolds the rod. It's an arrow. A steel arrow. She inserts the bottom of the arrow into her gun and adjusts it until there's a loud metallic click.

She holds out an arm to me, and I move closer to the woman in black. She puts an arm around my waist.

"You trust me?" she says.

I trust a handful of people. I don't know this woman. Even if she's who I think she is, I don't know her.

"Yes," I breathe.

"Then hold on."

I wrap my arms around her. She fires the gun at the ceiling. The arrow shoots upward, dragging a steel wire after it. The arrow hits its target. The woman is lifted off the ground. I gasp in shock as I go with her. Her arm is tight around my waist. I cling to the soft leather of her jacket.

"Don't look down," she says.

"I could have done this myself," I say. "I've got marbles."

"Marbles are fun," she says. "But there are times when a girl needs her mother."

The woman lands on a wooden beam. She reaches out to steady me and then she pushes upward. Above us, a skylight at the top of the gym opens. I see the gray Manhattan sky. It's not even dark yet. I feel like I've been in this nightmarish building for a week but I doubt it's been much more than an hour.

The woman climbs up through the skylight, turns, and reaches out a hand. I take it and allow myself to be yanked out of the gym.

Suddenly, I'm freezing. I see my breath in front of me. The late fall wind hits my face like an angry hand slapping me. I can also see office workers in cubicles in the building next to this one. That's because I'm standing on the ledge of the Dominion Brothers Building. The ledge of the forty-eighth floor.

"Remember I said don't look down?" the woman says. "Same thing applies here."

Up to this point in my life, I would have said I was not scared of heights. I would have said that because I have never before been this high. The stone ledge is maybe three feet wide. I plaster myself face-first against the cold concrete of the building.

"You can't stay here," says the woman. "You're a target for pigeon poop."

No sooner does she say those terrifying words than a white splotch hits the concrete wall mere inches from my face. I recoil in disgust.

The woman touches my hand.

"Come with me," she urges.

"Where are we going?" I moan.

"Somewhere safe," she says.

Her fingers circle my wrist. She leads me slowly around a corner.

"We just have to climb a little bit higher," she says. She lets go of my hand and starts up a metal ladder. My heart sinks. I remember how unsafe I felt climbing the rusty ladder to the roof of Reindeer Crescent Middle School a matter of months ago. Now I have to make it up to the forty-ninth floor of a huge concrete tower where gargoyles grin down at me as if they're anticipating the bloody mess I'll leave on the sidewalk when I tumble to my death.

"I get scared, too," the woman shouts back at me.

"Absolute wrong time to tell me that," I bawl up at her.

"But you know what I do to take my mind off it? I sing."

The wind is howling in my ears. The sounds of sirens screaming and car horns honking rise up from the streets below us. I hear the percussive sound of my teeth chattering. All that noise is swirling around my head, but as I climb the ladder, I hear the woman's soft voice. She sings, "If I could only win your love . . ."

Are you kidding me? I travel thousands of miles. I defeat a library filled with bad guys. I go face-to-face with a blond monster and now I'm trapped forty-eight-and-a-half stories up in the air with the Strangled Geese? How can this be the song she sings to banish her fear? This is no one's favorite song. Except for one person, and if it's his favorite song, it must be because it reminds him of her.

I look up at the short black skirt and the black boots and the black leather jacket of the woman making her way up the ladder. I watch her inky black hair whip around her shoulders. I know who she is.

I have a thousand things to say to her. I have another thousand things to ask her. But I can't do it right now because I have to follow her to the top of this endless ladder. So I start singing.

"If I could only win your love . . ."

# CHAPTER SEVENTEEN

# Irina 0

I'm forty-eight-and-a-half stories high and hanging onto a small metal ladder. The woman in black leans down and pushes her hand into the mouth of one of the gargoyles. The hideous stone creature swings away from the side of the building like it's about to take flight. But it doesn't take flight. It opens up to reveal a steel door.

"Not far now," the woman calls down to me. She unlocks the door and motions to me to clamber up the last few metal rungs and go inside.

Suddenly, I'm inside a spacious walk-in closet surrounded by shelves and drawers containing rows of clothes, shoes, and bags. The closet is big enough to contain two bamboo chairs and a large round mirror. The walls and ceiling are decorated in an orangey beige, or maybe it's a beigey orange. A few framed photographs are scattered around and there's a baby picture attached to the side of the mirror. The woman reaches down and opens a small white cabinet that turns out to be a mini-fridge. She takes out two cans of Sprite and hands me one.

"Bad for you," she says. "Rots your teeth. But just this once . . ."

The woman sinks into one of the bamboo chairs and gestures to me to do the same.

"Ahhh," she sighs as she relaxes into the chair.

I open the can and take a drink. It tastes amazing.

"What is this place?" I ask.

"My changing room," she says. "For when I need to grab a few things and go."

"It's nice." I smile. "I like the color."

"Butternut orange," she murmurs. "But that's not what you want to talk about."

"No." Now that I'm alone with her, now that I can ask her anything, I don't know where to start.

"My name is Irina Ouspenskaya," she says. "I was born in the Chechen Republic."

"Commonly known as Chechnya," I break in, eager to display my global knowledge. "Situated in the southernmost part of Eastern Europe, within a hundred kilometers of the Caspian Sea."

"Good Googling." She smiles. "Bad place. My family sought asylum in America in 1997. We moved to New Jersey. I went to high school and worked part-time for the King of Shish Kebab. Not the real king, the takeout one."

"But that was your cover, right?" I say. "You were a Chechen secret service agent?"

Irina grins and takes a gulp of Sprite. "Sometimes, a girl has to say things that aren't a hundred percent true to make herself seem interesting to a guy. This is very bad advice, by the way."

"Thanks, but—wait, you weren't an agent in high school?"

"I didn't fit in at John F. Kennedy High in Paterson. My English was not so good. The words made sense in my head but not when they came out my mouth. The other kids imitated me."

Like Brendan Chew! I seethe in silent sympathy for the young Irina.

"At home, my mother looked more like my grandmother and my grandmother looked like a pile of old dirty laundry; sorry to say, but it's the truth." She takes a sip of Sprite and looks lost in the memory. After a moment, she returns to her theme. "At the King of Shish Kebab, all I heard was, Asylum Girl, get me baba ghanoush. Asylum Girl, thicker slices. Asylum Girl, don't skimp on the hummus. Not the America I'd seen in the hip-hop videos. But one night, a boy comes into the King and he's different. He doesn't call me Asylum Girl, he doesn't throw money in my face or try to rob the cash register."

I see the connections forming. I know the guy.

"And he was thinner in those days," I say.

"No. Still fat. But funny and charming. And intriguing. Sometimes he'd come by two, three days in a row, then he'd be gone for weeks. One time, I ask him what he does for a living. He says, I'd tell you but I'd have to kill you."

"He's corny," I say, delighted at the image of Strike trying to act like he had any game.

"Quick as a flash, I tell him I know a lot more ways to kill than you do and I've got a lot more secrets." She gives me a shrug. "I have no idea where that came from."

I let out a Sprite-flavored burp, such is my shock. I see the connections forming and they're insane.

"Spies don't trust anyone," I yelp. "You made up something no one would believe, except the one guy who only believes the unbelievable. Why wouldn't the Asylum

Girl who worked for the King of Shish Kebab be under-cover? Weirder things have happened."

Irina nods. "One minute I had the most boring, most miserable, smelly life; the next Carter Strike was trying to get me to defect to his side and tell him all the dirty secrets I knew."

"Which you didn't," I say.

"Which I didn't." She agrees. "But he told me what an asset I could be to the CIA. He took me on missions. He taught me to fight, to shoot, to blend in, to observe, to vanish. And Irina Ouspenskaya, the asylum girl playing at being a spy, evolved into Irina O, real, actual spy."

She's a bigger liar than I am! I feel a lump in my throat. Fighting the urge to cry, I say, "What happened then?"

"There was a regime change in the CIA. The new team didn't trust the old guard. Strike was sent to South America on a job. He got abducted and I stopped hear-ing from him, which was a problem because by that time I found out I was going to be a mommy. An even bigger problem was that the new CIA team trusted me even less than Strike. I had another life to think about. So I got out. I traveled a little and then I had my beautiful baby on a stormy day in August."

"But you didn't keep her."

Irina closes her eyes. "I was a wild animal back then, Bridget," she says. "I thought Strike had been killed by the company we worked for. I thought I was next. I had to keep moving. I had to become like steel. I couldn't keep you. I wanted to but I couldn't."

Those big smudgy eyes stare into me, begging me to understand. I turn away from her and find myself looking at the baby picture tucked into the side of the mirror.

"It was like missing a limb," she says. "It never stopped hurting, but after a while I just accepted hurting as the only way I was ever going to feel. So I went back to work."

"For the CIA?" I ask.

She shakes her head. "For anyone who paid. For anyone who wanted jobs done that no one else would do."

"Did you kill people?"

"The world is not a less beautiful place without the presence of those I removed from it," she says.

"And that's what you do for the Forties," I say. "You're an assassin?"

"I was," she says. "Past tense. I'd had this feeling for a while that killing couldn't be the only thing I was awesome at. Maybe I could sing. . . ."

"I heard you sing," I say. "That's probably not going to work out as a long-term career choice."

"I heard you sing, too," she says, covering her ears and making an anguished face. "The point is, I needed to find something else to do. So I got out. But you don't just walk out on the Forties, not when you're their best, most in-demand hit woman. Edward Dominion begged me to come back. One more job, maybe two. Day and night: calls, texts, emails, gifts, cars, you name it."

"Did he buy you an ocelot?" I say.

"In butternut orange," she fires back. "But there's only one way an assassin's life ends."

"Someone better kills you," I say.

"Uh, there's no one better than Irina O, let's be clear about that," she says, and she looks deadly serious. "But my decision was final. I was not coming back to the Forties."

"Until . . . ," I prompt.

"Until Edward Dominion started messing with the lives of the people that mattered to me. Until he showed me how easy it was for him to find you and Strike. He gave me an ultimatum: come back to work, do one last job, or I'll keep tormenting them. I might even have done it. But that one last job . . ." She says nothing for a moment. "I don't eliminate children."

"Who . . . ?" I start to ask, hungry for more details. Irina doesn't reply. She springs up from the bamboo chair, goes over to the bottom drawer of the cabinet closest to her, and pulls out a black canvas messenger bag. Then she reaches out to the edge of a shelf lined with designer shoes. Irina gives the shelf a quick sharp pull. The entire shelving unit turns around. The clothes, bags, and shoes vanish into the wall. In their place are rows of weapons: guns, knives, arrows, grenades, small rubber things I don't know the names of, big curved metal things with ridged edges, basically lots of stuff designed to cause maximum damage.

Irina walks up and down the shelves, casting an expert eye on her armory, stopping to pick up a gun or a knife or a rubber thing and either throw it into her canvas bag or return it to its resting place.

"When you said this was your changing room, you weren't kidding."

"Nope," she says.

I watch my biological mother slide a knife into a hidden space in the heel of her boot. I watch her wind a length of steel wire around her fist and then place it carefully in the bag.

"So, um, what's happening now?" I ask.

"What's happening is, I'm getting you as far away from this place as possible, and then I'm coming back and blowing it to pieces."

"What about Strike?" I say.

"What about him?"

"Don't we need to get him far away from this place, too?"

"He's a big boy," Irina says. "He can figure his own way out."

"I visited him at his place," I tell her. "He was eating a chicken with his bare hands. I asked him why. He said he couldn't be bothered washing his fork. He has one fork! No wonder he was so easy to put in a crate!"

"I can't help everyone," says Irina, as if I were tugging at her sleeve and peppering her with annoying questions. Strike's not everyone! I give her my most outraged stare, but she busies herself filling her bag with bombs and weird plastic brick things.

My ringtone sounds. I think, *I promise, I'll wear a scarf!*

**It's not my** mother. Surveillance camera feed appears on my screen. The Squirrel again?

This footage is clearer. A few people standing in a large room nodding. Alex Gunnery, little Lucien, and Joanna. No Sam. The camera moves to show the person they're nodding at. A tall, distinguished man with white hair. Behind him, the windows in the room give a panoramic view of the office building opposite. The same view I had when I was standing out on the ledge. Joanna and the Gunnerys must be on the forty-eighth floor. I check the time code. They didn't go home. They're here right now. But who is that white-haired man?

"That's Edward Dominion," says Irina, looking over my shoulder.

At the sound of his name, the man on my phone looks straight at the camera and smiles.

# CHAPTER EIGHTEEN

# *Bad Plan*

Irina and I watch Edward Dominion as he talks to Alex Gunnery, Joanna, and little Lucien. Alex is nodding and making big elaborate hand gestures.

"Wow, that woman's got a lot of scarves," says Irina.

I remember how soft they felt the first time she hugged me.

"He's going to hang her with them," says Irina.

"Don't say that!" I shout. "That's my best friend's aunt and her cousin."

"Well, I hope you took a lot of nice photos to remember them because they're not getting out of here."

There's no emotion on her face. No fear or concern.

"Their best bet is he decides to recruit them, but their lives are still over." She shrugs.

"We have to help them," I say.

She shakes her head. "That would be playing into Edward's hands. And anyway, are you a hundred percent sure it's even them?"

"Of course, I'm sure," I say. "I've known Joanna since I was . . ." And then I remember the man with Strike's face. I remember the nanomasks. I stare at the phone.

"No," I say. "It's them. Who are they going to find to substitute for a little five-year-old boy?"

"A kung fu dwarf," she replies without even a second's hesitation.

"Do they have those?" I ask.

"On floor forty two and a half," she says. "But you're right, it's probably them."

"So what's the plan?"

"Same as five minutes ago," she says. "Get you out of here, then blow up the Forties."

"Bad plan," I say. "I'm the reason Alex and Joanna and little Lucien are in Edward Dominion's clutches. My lies brought them here."

Irina gives me a fond look. "We're a lot alike." She goes to touch my hand.

"We're clearly not," I say, snatching it away. "If you feel something for me and you want to protect me, you have to want to protect them, too, even if you don't care about them."

She lets out a frustrated sigh. "This is what he wants. To pull us apart. To make me vulnerable so he can control me again."

"Stay here, then," I say. "But I can't."

I climb on top of a cabinet and start to open the secret compartment that leads to the outside of the building. Irina pulls me back down. I struggle out of her arms. She gives me a furious glare.

"You want me to go save these people I don't know," she says, the accent of her native land becoming more pronounced. "Fine. I'll do it for you."

She grabs her black canvas bag of weapons and jumps on top of the cabinet. This time I pull her back.

"Bad plan," I say. "That's what he's expecting. He'll have a hundred armed goons lying in wait for you."

"Only a hundred." Irina fake yawns. "I'm insulted."

"What he's not expecting is that the mama lion, i.e., you, would be careless enough to let her favorite cub, i.e., me, wander unprotected into . . . I was going to say the lion's den, but that's one too many lion references. . . . What I mean is, he won't be expecting me to show up."

"No," she says. "No way."

"Think about it," I persist. "He wants you but he'll be interested in me. He doesn't need Alex, Joanna, and the kung fu dwarf. He lets them go. You spirit them to safety. Maybe you could pretend to be a tour guide. I act like I'm amazed and enthralled by the whole one-stop-shopping empire he's built here. I'll tell him it's the Amazon of crime. It's Crimeazon."

"Not that funny," sniffs Irina.

"He'll find it charming," I assure her. "I'm the unexpected factor in this equation. And I'll make him think I can win you back to the Forties, because we had an instant connection."

"That's something you're making up for Edward or you think we have an instant connection?" says Irina.

I'm starting to get a clearer picture of my biological mother, and it's not what I expected. Irina Ouspenskaya is an insecure person, trying to impress me with her assassin's prowess one minute, worrying what I think of her the next. It makes her seem more human. It makes me like her.

"Of course we do," I say.

Her face lights up, as much a face as pale as a street covered in newly fallen snow can light up. "So I whisk the scarves woman, the dwarf, and the other one . . ."

"Her name's Joanna," I point out.

". . . Joanna to safety while you spin a web of lies to

Edward Dominion, and then . . ."

"Then Irina O builds a ladder of broken bones for me to walk down and out of the Dominion Brothers Building."

Irina reaches out and touches my cheek. "A ladder of broken bones," she whispers, and I swear, I see her eyes grow damp.

**She guides me** out of her secret changing room and toward an elevator on the forty-ninth floor. As the door opens, she gives me a quick hug, and I feel her hand slipping something into my pocket.

"Bad plan," she murmurs into my ear. "But you're doing it for the right reasons. Just remember I'm close if it all goes haywire."

I step inside the elevator. I see mirrors and shiny gold buttons. I instantly relax, swipe Gunnery's key card, and reach out to press forty-eight.

Twelve seconds later, I walk out onto a floor with a deep, rich red carpet and white walls lined on both sides with big burly black-clad guys holding weapons and staring dead ahead. They make no sound and no eye contact.

"I'm here to see Sir Edward Dominion." Did I just say *sir*? "Edward Dominion. I'm Bridget Wilder. Of the Sacramento Wilders."

The massive gentleman closest to me jerks a thumb to the end of the floor, where two large white doors are flanked by security guards. I begin my silent walk toward the white doors. And then I hear my phone ring. I look at my phone.

Dad. Not Carter Strike. My dad dad.

"If I can make it there, I'll make it anywhere, it's up to you, New York, New Yoooork," he sings down the phone. I glance left and right at the double line of deadly Dominion security men while listening to my father's full-throated performance.

"Are you okay?" I ask, after he finally lets go of the showstopper last note. "Did you eat some bad bacon? Because it sounded like you were being violently sick."

"Where are the pictures?" Dad says. "That was part of our deal: we let you visit Joanna in New York City and you keep us entertained with a constant supply of pictures showing us where you are and what you're doing on your fun trip."

I curse silently. I had ample opportunities to send pictures from the airport and the SUV, pictures of happy smiling Gunnerys, pictures of the amazing exterior and even more amazing interior of the Dominion Brothers Building.

"I put Ryan in charge of visuals," I lie.

"He sends me six-second clips of dogs pooping on the sidewalk," Dad says. "It gets old after the first twenty."

"I'll be sure and rectify the situation."

"Rectify it right now," Dad says. "Where are you? What are you doing? Have you eaten the famous New York pizza? Is it better than ours?"

I glance up. Where I am is halfway up the long corridor. The massed ranks of security guards stare over my head.

"No pizza yet. I'm . . . we're just walking around," I reply in a way that hopefully communicates my desire for this conversation to be at an end.

"Don't forget. I want pictures," he says.

I'm about to end the call when I have the sudden urge to keep talking. Hearing my dad's voice takes my mind off my current situation and the gun-toting security giants on either side of me.

"What's going on at home?" I say. "How's Natalie doing without me and Ryan overshadowing her with our amazing accomplishments?"

"Big cheer crisis," replies Dad, in hushed tones to communicate the gravity of the situation. "The Cheerminators didn't qualify for the Cheer Classic. The Blue Canyon somethings . . ."

"Bronze Canyon Valkyries?"

"Yeah, them. They made it. Your sister is not happy. Heads are rolling."

I don't want to end the call.

"Hey, Dad, what's happening on *Law & Order*?" I ask.

"Bridget." He laughs. "You did not fly to New York so you could ask me about a TV show."

"I learned a lot from that show," I find myself insisting as I creep farther up the corridor. "It taught me that no matter how tough the bad guys are, how many weapons they have, and how well protected they think they are"—I look at the security men to my left and my right—"they can't escape justice."

On the phone, my dad starts recapping the last episode he watched.

"Uh-huh," I say, not really listening. I feel comfortable walking down the double line of brutal killers while my dad talks in my ear. Finally, I reach the white double doors.

"That sounds great," I say. "We'll watch a marathon when I get back."

I end the call.

A guard pushes one door open and I walk inside.

# CHAPTER NINETEEN

# This Charming Man

A heavy red velvet curtain faces me once I walk through the door and into the room. I take a few cautious steps forward, reach out my hand, and push through the curtain. On the other side, I see a very fancy sitting room, complete with grand piano, chandelier, and rubber tree plants climbing halfway to the ceiling. Alex and Joanna sit on luxurious armchairs. Little Lucien sprawls out in the middle of his chair, a wheezy snore noise emerging from his open mouth every few seconds. He's clearly crashed from the heights of his Bridget-instigated sugar high. Alex and Joanna both have little tables set up next to their chairs. Each table is piled high with a selection of sandwiches, cakes, and tea. On the wall, a sixty-inch TV shows black-and-white footage of the building's historic opening night. Edward Dominion sits, sipping from a teacup, in front of windows that show his stunning view of the city. He is the first to see me enter the room.

"Bridget Wilder," he says, standing up.

"Sir Edward," I say. Why do I keep calling him Sir Edward? "I mean, Mr. Dominion."

"B!" sings out Alex Gunnery. "Where have you been? Edward's been such an amazing host."

"I'll bet he has." I give Edward Dominion a cold *I know who you are and what you're about* stare.

In return, he gives me a big beaming smile.

"It's my absolute pleasure," says Edward Dominion.

"Oh, no, it's ours," sighs Alex. She's looking at Edward—his perfect dark blue pinstriped suit, his immaculate white hair, his tanned features and kind smile—like he's a rare and precious jewel. Getting her out of here might be a tough job.

"Bridget," says Edward. "Come join us, please. I only wish you'd gotten here earlier so I could have shared a little of my family history with you."

Am I imagining a little half smirk when he's saying

this? Like he's actually saying, *Murder is my business and business is booming.*

"Where's Sam?" Joanna suddenly says. "Wasn't he with you?"

I give her a grateful smile. Just the cue I need.

"He's downstairs," I say. "He's ready to go. Me too. He sent me up to get you."

"Bring the boy up," says Edward.

"He's seen enough for today," I say. "He doesn't want to impose."

"Nonsense." Edward grins. Another victim in my clutches.

"Go get him, Bridget," pipes up Joanna. I give her a sharp look, counting on our years of friendship to make her see that I'm trying to communicate my urgent need to get her out of this lovely room. But Joanna only has eyes for the huge heapings of baked goods sitting in front of her.

She turns back to the mountain of food on her table and selects a red velvet cake.

"Perhaps we have taken up too much of your time," says Alex.

"Not another word about leaving," says Edward, smiling at her. "It's rare I get a firsthand chance to talk about the history of this building. We've had so many visitors over the decades. Late at night I can almost feel their presence in the walls and"—he looks directly at me—"deep under the ground."

Okay. That was a threat.

I charge forward, yank the cake out of Joanna's mouth, and pull her to her feet.

"Ah woo gowa mawa pwawa," she splutters. She swallows the half of the cake that's still in her mouth and gives me a deadly stare.

"Sorry," I say. "But we have to go now."

"I think you're being very rude, Bridget," says Alex.

"That's just how she is," says Joanna, a familiar edge entering her voice. "She's completely rude and thoughtless. Everything has to be about her. She couldn't just come to visit a friend. We have to go where she wants to go and then leave when she wants."

"Oh my God, Joanna," I wail. "You're bringing this up now?"

"Bridget's got a lot of important secrets," Joanna announces to Alex, who looks mortified, and to Edward, who seems amused. "She only lets you know what she wants you know."

Here's the Joanna I know. Here's all the venom and built-up resentment I thought I missed.

Her face is reddening as her eyes narrow. I feel a fight

coming on. This is not the time or place. I need to shut her up and make her listen. I reach out to the table, grab a cupcake, and shove it into her open mouth.

"Bridget!" I hear an aghast Alex shout.

"Bwwiwww," I hear a furious Joanna try to shout.

I pull Joanna close, wrapping my hands around her forearms and leaning in to her ear. "This is a trap," I say, my voice soft but bristling with authority. "Get Alex and Lucien out of here or he'll hurt them. Sam already knows. You can hate me all you want, but you know I'm on your side. So go."

I take a step back. Joanna stares at me, her mouth still stuffed with cake. She swallows it in one gulp, goes over to the sleeping Lucien, picks him up, and slings him over her shoulder.

"The little monster needs to go home," Joanna says to Alex.

Alex watches Joanna head toward the red curtain. She gives Edward a regretful gaze.

"I'm so sorry," she sighs.

"Children," says Edward. "The joy they bring to our lives balances out the chaos."

"I'll try to remember that," she says. "Thank you again for today."

"My pleasure," he says.

He escorts her toward the curtain.

"Sir Ed . . ." I curse myself and start again. "Mr. Dominion, before I go, can I ask you a question? It's for school."

"Of course, Bridget," he says.

Alex turns back to me. She could not dislike me more at this moment and I don't blame her. I'm responsible for kicking her out of this wonderful unexpected afternoon with the dreamiest rich man in the world, and now I'm attempting to monopolize his attention.

"You go ahead," I tell her. "I'll catch up."

"Can't wait for that," she says sourly, and vanishes through the curtain.

"Tell your men to stand down," I say to Edward.

"Already done," he says, and directs me to an armchair. "We'll be left alone."

He sits opposite me, crossing one leg over the other and reaching for his teacup.

"I don't really have a question for school," I tell him.

"I know," he says. "You're stalling for time while your birth mother makes sure your friend and her family get safely out of the building. That's not an Irina plan. You persuaded her to do things your way, which is something I haven't been able to accomplish with any great success."

Wow. He read me like a book with six pages, no

words, and pictures of cows wearing yellow boots, i.e., a book that's pitifully easy to read.

"You're an impressive young woman, Bridget," he goes on. "You're resourceful, you're loyal, and you're fearless. These are attributes I don't often come across in people your age."

I know he's the ruthless boss of a secret crime empire, but Dominion's got this charm thing about him. He makes me feel like the most important person in the world, and I can't help it: I'm flattered.

"I'm afraid to say I look at young people today and there's a sense of entitlement, even when it's not merited. I always wondered how Irina's daughter would turn out, and I'm impressed. You're not afraid to put in hard work to achieve your objectives. I admire that about you."

I bask in the glow of his admiration for a few seconds, and then I remember why I'm here. It is not to bask.

"How long have you known she had a daughter?"

Edward purses his lips. "How long has she worked here? Four, no, five years."

"And she told you about me five years ago?" I say.

He shakes his head. "She said nothing. Not a word to anyone. But I had her phones and computers monitored. I was aware of every secret little detour she took to Sacramento to hide in the shadows and watch you and your adopted family."

"What?" is all I can say. This isn't like Strike showing up in the nick of time to try and save me from Section 23. Irina's been lingering on the outskirts of my life for five years?

"Look at it from her point of view," says Edward, once again reading me like a book. "She wanted to see that you were happy and that you were being cared for by good people who loved you. Her presence in your life at that stage would only have upset everybody. You were part of a family structure that had no place for her. That's why she always came back to the family structure that did have a place for her. Here in the Forties, where she belongs."

Edward leans toward me. "You could have a place here, too."

I'm lost in my thoughts. Was Irina there when I tried out for ballet class and broke my toe? Was she there at the Christmas party when my mother made me sit next to Joanna for the first time? During our family trips to Raging Waters? Just watching?

"Wait, what?" I splutter. "Did you say something about me having a place here, too?"

Edward takes a sip from his teacup and nods. "You've got a lot of potential."

"Not a compliment," I say shrilly. "You sell the services of the scum of the earth." I remember Irina was one of those scum. "With some exceptions," I add.

"I don't like that negative way of thinking," he says. "I assembled a variety of professionals under one roof and made hiring them efficient and affordable. If it wasn't for me, Irina would be out there running wild, making enemies like she was before I recruited her. If we work together, you and I, we can keep her safe. More tea?"

Before I can reply, he pours me a cup. I take it from him. Edward Dominion is a man who knows how to get what he wants. When he speaks, I feel myself being molded like clay.

What am I thinking? Edward Dominion is every bit as evil as the thugs, villains, crooks, conmen, and killers who work for him. In fact, he's more evil because he uses his powers of persuasion to make you think you're doing something good when he's really making you do the exact opposite.

"That's a shame," he sighs before I've uttered a word. "Because now lines have formed. From Irina to you to Jeff and Nancy and Ryan and Natalie and Alex and Joanna and Sam and . . ."

He throws his hands in the air. "It goes on and on. You see how Irina's life impacts so many? If she stays and does the jobs she owes me, all your friends and family members carry on with their little lives in blissful ignorance. If she goes, they all go."

He flutters his hand in the air as if to demonstrate how disposable the lives of others are to him.

My head is exploding. He knows my mom and dad's names. He knows Ryan and Natalie. He knows everything.

"Pretty powerful motivation to change Irina's mind, wouldn't you say?" He smiles at me.

I'm incapable of arguing with him. He knows what I'm going to say before I've even thought it. He sees the big picture and all I see is—all I see is the window behind him shatter.

Edward jumps from his seat and pulls a gun from inside his jacket. He starts shooting but the bullets smash into concrete.

The window was broken by a gargoyle. The same clawed, winged, concrete demon that guards the ledges of the building's upper tower is now hurtling through the broken window and into Edward's luxurious room. It smashes straight into him, knocking him onto his back.

Of course, the gargoyle did not fly in here using its concrete wings. The statue was thrown in here by the guy who leaps in after it and is now sitting on top of it, completely flattening and immobilizing Edward Dominion.

Carter Strike.

# CHAPTER TWENTY

# Tea and No Sympathy

"Strike!" I yelp in disbelief.

"Strike," groans Edward, the combined weight of my biological father and a concrete gargoyle pressing down on his chest.

"You okay?" Strike asks.

"I am now," I say.

"I'm not," moans Edward.

"That's the plan," says Strike. He looks over at the table of cakes and sandwiches.

"Can I get a cake, Bridget?" he asks "I'm dying for something sweet." I carry a whole plate of cakes over to him. He shuffles down the back of the gargoyle, making room for me near the head. I pass Strike the plate and sit down next to him. I hear Edward gasp in pain underneath us. The gargoyle's head is barely an inch from his face. Strike picks up a round pink-and-white delicacy.

"What's this?" he asks.

"Raspberry and almond, I think," I say.

He takes a bite. "Mmmm," he moans. "What are you having?"

I hold up a brown slice. "Chocolate caramel."

"Nice," he says.

"Would you like some tea, Mr. Strike?" I ask with exaggerated formality.

"Tea would be a delight," he replies in similar fashion.

I hop off the gargoyle and pour a cup, which I present to Strike. He brings the cup to his mouth, blows on it, then takes a sip.

"Hits the spot," he sighs.

He drinks his tea and wolfs down his cake. I plow through my slice. It's a nice warm moment between us, the sort we haven't had in a while. I feel safe with him sitting next to me.

"I guess Sam found you," I say.

"Who?" he replies.

"Alex's son."

"Who?" he says again.

"Didn't he have Red with him?"

"I don't understand one word you're saying," he says.

I groan in frustration. "That jerkface. I told him to . . . and he didn't even . . . and he took . . . I'm sorry, I tried to send someone to help you. But I guess you didn't need help."

"I appreciate the thought," he says between mouthfuls of cake. "But you shouldn't have come here."

I swallow my creamy confection and stare at him. "Are you kidding? You send me those texts and then you vanish."

Strike winces. "Give me a do-over. What I meant was, I'm glad you're here and you're okay and this is fun, we should definitely do this more often. I should get the recipes for these cakes before we go. But I know the lies you had to tell to get here, and that's not something I want on my conscience. Your parents have been great to me. We need to be as straight with them as we can under the circumstances."

"Those texts," I say. "And then my mom's van showing up outside your building."

"I had a gut feeling something bad was about to happen," he says. "I just didn't move fast enough. It won't happen again."

"You're dead, Strike," Edward shouts in a raspy,

strangled voice. "I've got nine floors of criminals who won't hesitate to kill you."

Strike sips a little tea. "Incorrect, your majesty," he says, glancing down at the red-faced man trapped under the gargoyle. "You've got nine floors of criminals who became criminals because they never wanted to work for a boss, which is what you are. You've kept them here through a mixture of persuasion and intimidation. The moment one of them sees you lying down there in that embarrassing position, any hold you have on them will be gone and this place will be the empty shell it used to be. They might even steal your expensive shoes before they go."

"That's . . ." Edward doesn't finish the sentence. As always, he sees the big picture and he knows Strike's right.

I turn back to face Strike. "How was the journey in the crate?"

"Not that bad." He shrugs. "I've been in tighter spots. How was the journey in the plane?"

I shudder. "The worst, most uncomfortable, most annoying experience of my life."

"I haven't been to New York for a while," he says.

"Not since you used to order takeout from the King of Shish Kebab?" I say.

"Ah," he murmurs. "Okay. I wondered . . ."

We fall silent for a moment. Should I wait for him to ask me about Irina? Did he even know she was still alive? Have they been in contact since he met me? Did he know she was never really in the Chechen secret service?

"Oh, for God's sake," wheezes Edward. "You both have questions. Ask them. Say what's on your mind."

"He always knows," I marvel.

"That's how you get to be a criminal mastermind," says Strike. He finishes his tea in one slurp, inhales, and then breathes out. "Okay. The elephant in the room. I know you've met . . ."

He doesn't finish his sentence. He doesn't get a chance.

A steel arrow flies up over the shards of glass still standing in the window frame. The arrow embeds itself high in the wall above the gargoyle. A steel wire stretches out. Strike jumps off the gargoyle and positions himself in front of me. Irina comes hurtling through the window, gun in hand. She lets go and lands in the middle of the room. She looks at me and relief floods her pale face. She takes in the gargoyle and the flattened figure of Edward underneath. Then she looks at Strike.

If it were possible, I'd say she just turned whiter.

"You always knew how to make an entrance," he smiles. The smile fades and he inhales sharply.

Irina puts a hand over her mouth. Her eyes widen in shock. I follow her gaze. The sleeve of Strike's jacket has been torn away. The white shirt underneath has a red stain on the upper arm and that stain is getting bigger.

"The arrow," she gasps. "I'm sorry."

"Flesh wound." He shrugs. Then he pulls a ragged tissue from his pocket and attempts to stop the flow of blood.

"Let me," Irina says. She pulls off her leather jacket and ties it around his upper arm.

"And they say romance is dead," groans Edward. "Girl wounds boy, girl tends boy's wounds, and then they kiss."

Irina looks up at Strike as she tightens the jacket around his arm. He looks back at her.

Oh my God! They want to! They totally want to!

Ewwww!

# CHAPTER TWENTY-ONE

# Meet the Parents

Irina shoves Strike away and slaps the arm she didn't wound with her arrow-shooting gun thing.

"Fourteen years," she says.

"I wish it had been longer," he replies.

They don't want to. They totally don't want to!

I remain sitting on the gargoyle, watching the awkward interaction between my biological parents.

"You deserve so much more than an arrow through the arm," snarls Irina. "After what you did to me."

Strike's mouth falls open. He slaps a palm against his forehead. "What I did to you?"

"I was a naive, trusting immigrant girl," she yells. "You left me alone. You took off without a word."

"You lied to the new management," Strike shouts back. "You told them I was a double agent."

I stare at Irina. "You left that small part out when you were telling me the story of your life."

Irina squirms. "It happened so long ago. I don't remember every little detail."

Strike's face reddens. "You turned on me to save your butt when the new bosses came in."

"Well, it didn't work," Irina snaps. "They never trusted me, not for a minute. I was always in fear for my life and that of my beautiful baby's." Irina reaches out to touch my cheek. I turn my head from her. Suddenly, the thought that I have inherited Irina's lying gene is filling with me horror. The lines start to connect.

"If you hadn't lied about Strike, the CIA wouldn't have sent him away," I say. "He would have known you were having a baby. He would have known about me."

Irina bows her head so her hair falls over her face and I can't see her expression. I hear her murmur, "That's a lot of ifs. You don't know it would have worked out like that."

"You're sure you want to give up hurting people for a living, Irina?" says Edward from underneath the gargoyle. "You're so good at it."

Strike sits down next to me and puts his non-wounded arm over my shoulder. "Irina and I have our differences, Bridget, but you can't blame her for us not being a family. We were different people. Those were different times. Everybody lied, no one trusted anyone, everybody stabbed everybody else in the back."

"So how were they different times?" I say.

"Because I've never lied to you," says Strike. "And I never will."

We both look at Irina. Black tears are dribbling down her pale face.

"Don't cry," I say.

"I'm not," she gasps.

"Tear gas!" yells Strike. He points to the red velvet curtain. A second tear gas grenade rolls into view, joining the first one.

Edward laughs and weeps at the same time. "Your observation that my employees would desert me in my time of need? Care to think again? They were waiting until I had the whole family under my roof."

Strike throws his elbow over his face.

"Get Bridget out of here," he tells Irina.

"Bridget's fought her way out of worse situations than this," I say as I reach for my box of marbles.

From the other side of the curtain we hear the sound of feet charging toward us. The floor shakes. It sounds like a lot of feet.

Irina yanks at the steel wire attached to her arrow and winds it back into her gun.

"Let's go," she says to me.

Strike kicks the gargoyle off Edward and pulls him to his feet.

"Human shield?" says Irina.

"It'll buy you some time." He nods.

"Okay, wait, let's not be hasty," Edward chimes in. "This doesn't have to end in bloodshed."

"It won't for me," Strike says.

"Find us," says a choked-up Irina. "We'll wait for you."

"I'll meet you in the safe house," gasps Strike as the tear gas fills the room, making it impossible to see or speak.

I feel Irina wrap her arms around me. I feel the wind in my face as we leave the building and then I feel myself fly through the air.

"Don't drop me!" I hear myself scream.

"I let you go once," Irina yells back. "I won't do it again."

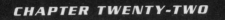

# CHAPTER TWENTY-TWO

# Safe House

We're in Chinatown. Around me, I see food vendors packing up their stalls for the night. Wooden tables groan with knock-off handbags and T-shirts. One of the men behind the tables sees me staring in his direction. "Gucci, Prada, Chanel!" he shouts. "Buy something nice. The boys will like you better if you don't look like a fool."

"You look like a fool!" I shout back, enraged. (Actually, I do look like a fool. I'm wearing an I Love New York sweatshirt and a green foam Statue of Liberty crown. So is Irina. Her idea. Apparently, we're safer if we blend in.)

Irina slips her arm through mine and tugs me away. We walk under scaffolding, passing an electronics store, a Buddhist temple, and a restaurant with roasted ducks and chickens hanging on skewers in the window. The smell wafting out is amazing. I slow down, starving, but Irina speeds up, yanking me along in her wake. She takes a sharp left turn and charges down a grimy alley. Here, the smell is not amazing. Black garbage bags swollen to the point of bursting litter the alley. Angry cats hiss and spit in the darkness, cursing us for invading their unpleasant home turf.

Cats aren't the only inhabitants of this dark, dirty place. I hear a familiar scampering, the same pattering of tiny feet I became acquainted with when I was stuck in an air vent trying to escape from Section 23.

So, rats, we meet again.

Suddenly, Irina stops walking and digs into her pocket. We're outside a door with peeling black paint. She pulls out a key and sticks it in a padlock.

"Go on," she says, ushering me through the open door.

Last time she did this, I went from the outside of a concrete tower into a warm and welcoming little oasis of calm and comfort. This time, I fumble around in the dark for a moment before a light goes on and I'm immediately reminded of all the times my dad didn't get to watch sports or *L&O* because Mom was immersed in a program about people who live in quaint old country farmhouses. This kitchen, with its shelves filled with jars of jam, honey, and sugar, would make my mom moan with envy. Irina turns on more lights. I follow her through a hallway filled with vases of freshly cut flowers and a bamboo umbrella stand into a living room that groans with antique furniture and mountains of throw pillows. It's a room designed for comfort and relaxation, but Irina is pacing the floor like a panther.

I sink into the couch and make a fun fort out of the many, many pillows.

"Can you sit down and talk to me?" I say, feeling a little like the adult in this situation. "I get that you're on edge but you're making me tense, too."

Irina plops down next to me. Her eyes are darting from her watch to the living room door and back to me.

"I feel very safe here in the safe house," I say. "I thought places like this were bare-bones and only used for emergencies, but I could vacation in here. I bet all the other assassins want to hang out at Irina O's."

"It's not for me," she says. "Sometimes the people I was assigned to erase didn't deserve to be erased. Not a lot of times, but sometimes. So I brought them here and arranged for them to disappear."

"Oh," I say again.

"So I'm not quite the villain you think I am."

I'm about to protest when she says, "But I am a bad guy. I did lie about Strike to save myself and I probably did ruin any chance of us ever being a family."

Irina gets up and goes over to a shelf filled with figurines. She begins arranging and rearranging them.

"A real bad guy wouldn't have checked up on me," I say.

Irina turns back to face me, a china clown nestling in her palm. "I wanted to know you were with good people. That you were happy and healthy and living the life I wanted for you."

"I was," I say. "I am. They're the best. Well, Ryan's kind of a tool."

"I can't believe he got away with stealing the red fox from the zoo," she says.

"Right?" I say, amazed. "Wait, you knew about that?"

"Spy." She shrugs.

Irina suddenly lets out a little gasp and lets go of the china clown. I watch it fall to the ground and smash.

"Irina?" I say, scared. I jump off the couch and run to her.

Irina's eyes roll up in her head. Her legs buckle and

she collapses onto the floor, where she lies motionless.

"What's wrong?" I shout.

The air behind Irina starts to ripple. A shape forms, transparent at first; then it becomes whole.

A girl not much older than me, with blond, sideswept hair, wearing a black cocktail dress, stands over the still body of Irina Ouspenskaya brandishing a syringe.

She holds both palms up to me and smirks. "The wrong hands," she says in an upper-class English accent. *Who is this? Where did she come from? And why is she acting like she knows me?*

"She's not dead. In case you were worried," the girl goes on. "She'll be good as new tomorrow. She might drool a little. She may also have trouble swallowing or blinking or remembering her name, but other than that, she'll be in tip-top condition."

I can't form words. All I can do is stare and shake with fright. The more terrified I am, the more poised and amused the girl seems.

"Give me your tired, your poor, your huddled masses yearning to breathe free," she solemnly intones.

I must look baffled because she points to the top of my head and smirks, "That's a good look for you."

I'm still wearing my stupid foam Statue of Liberty crown! And my I Love New York hoodie! I go to pull the crown off my head but then I stop. Something about this girl strikes a familiar chord. Her high heels give her a few inches, her eyes are blue instead of gray, her lipstick-reddened mouth is bigger, and her voice is different, but I know this girl.

"Bl—Blabby?"

CHAPTER TWENTY-THREE

# *The Intern*

"**B**eing an intern sucks," the girl with the English accent says with feeling as she steps over the body of my birth mother and walks toward me. I take a few stumbling steps backward until I bang into the couch and I can't help but sit down. I stare up at this blond girl with the syringe and the cold smile who doesn't look anything like Ryan's silent, freakishly annoying girlfriend, Abby Rheinhardt. So why can't I shake the feeling that it is her?

"Do this, go here, clean this up, take this away, call this number, pick up my lunch," she says, as if we're in the middle of a conversation. "That's all you're there for.

No one knows your name, no one notices you, no one says thank you. But the upside is, you get to spend time on every floor of the Forties. When no one notices you, no one knows what you're learning, what you're reading, what you're overhearing, or what you're stealing." She wiggles the syringe at me. "Trusted agents with years of experience need their department heads to approve of them being issued a single vial of the cloaking liquid. I stole a few teaspoons here and there. Not enough that anyone would miss."

She lets out a melodic trilling laugh. I hug a cushion to stop myself from trembling.

"Y-you're her. You're Abby. Aren't you?"

The blond girl looks down at her long red nails, then gives me a pitying smile.

"Look at your little peanut-shaped head straining to understand. Don't give yourself an aneurysm, Bridget. The name I used under the terms of the agreement was Abigail Rheinhardt. And Abigail Rheinhardt was a very good, very obedient intern and, not to toot Abby's horn, a very, very quick study. She learned from the hackers, the gangsters, the leakers, the con artists, the kidnappers, the bank robbers, the blackmailers, the home invaders, the hired muscle, and the assassins. And she picked up a few skills of her own: she became a chameleon. She could adapt her look, her posture, her accent. She could become an entirely different person. All of which, you might think, would result in Abigail Rheinhardt rising up the ranks from intern to full-fledged employee of the Forties."

I glance past the scarily calm and articulate blond English girl to see if there are any signs of life in Irina's body. Nothing. Not even a twitch. I feel a sudden pain shoot up my big toe. The girl kicked me! I stare up at her.

"Shall I continue?" She shoots me a dirty look like I'm the rude one! "Thanks so much. Abigail Rheinhardt did, in fact, get her richly deserved promotion. What was her important, world-altering first mission? I'll tell you: she was sent to a bland, boring suburb in California to mess with the life of a painfully average middle school student."

I wonder if I know the poor unfortunate victim she's talking about. Then I realize I do.

"Oh," I say. The dots start to connect. This posh blond nightmare pretended to be Ryan's girlfriend to get access to me and to my family. She was the one who framed me by sending Cheerminator choreography to the Bronze Canyon Valkyries. She was the one who invited the world to a fake party on the same day as Casey Break-bush's birthday. She was in my house. She kissed my brother. She was in his room. She was probably in all of our rooms. And she poured soda on my laptop. But why? My head is about to explode. Her invasion of my privacy is beyond anything I can comprehend.

"You" is all I manage to get out.

"Aw, peanut." She wrinkles her nose at me. "I could have done so much more, you don't even know. I had such elaborate plans for you. There was going to be a cyberbullying scandal. I was going to steal from your father's employees and plant the evidence in your backpack. Neighborhood pets would have been abducted and you would have been exposed as the evil head of an animal smuggling ring. I would have turned your funny little family against you. Honestly, you would have been a pariah living in a cardboard box by the time I was through. I would have done a smashing job."

She sighs at the thought of this missed opportunity.

"But the program was accelerated. The orders were to forget you and concentrate on Strike."

"So you stole my mom's van and . . ."

"You would think I had earned that level of responsibility," she says, nodding at me. "But no. My job was apparently done. All I was considered capable of were missions involving idiot teenagers or whatever you are. Do you even qualify as a tween?" She says the word *tween* like she just smelled something rancid.

"I'm almost fourteen," I say.

"Almost," the blonde smirks, and then returns to her story. "And that's when I realized: I can follow the rules, I can excel, I can work hard in silence and hope someday my worth is recognized. Or I can take what's mine."

The blond girl puts a hand on her hip and strikes a dramatic pose.

"All my father cares about is getting Irina Ouspenskaya to do the one last job she owes him, so I'm going to do it myself and he's going to see what he's been taking for granted all these years."

"Wait, what, I'm sorry," I say. "Your father?"

"Oh, didn't I say? How rude of me." She lifts her chin and straightens her shoulders. "I'm Vanessa Dominion."

# CHAPTER TWENTY-FOUR

# Broken Home

E dward Dominion's daughter was in my home. Edward Dominion's daughter dated my brother. Edward Dominion's daughter turned people against me. Edward Dominion's daughter stuck a needle in my birth mother, who is now lying on the floor showing no signs of life.

"And now I bet you're wondering what Edward Dominion's daughter is going to do to you," says Vanessa, showing she has her father's irritating talent for anticipating reactions.

"Actually, I'm not," I say. "I'm Carter Strike's

daughter, and last time I looked, Carter Strike was using your father as a human shield. But that was the last time I looked. There probably isn't enough of him left to make an effective shield by now."

Vanessa shrugs. "You're asking me to shed tears over a man who dumped me in an English private school ten seconds after my first pee. Not for a moment am I worried about Edward Dominion. But if I were you, I'd worry about Carter Strike. My father thinks three steps ahead of his enemies. That's why he's still alive and they're either dead or working for him."

"Carter Strike threw him under a gargoyle and then sat on top of it," I shout back.

Vanessa smooths back her hair, smiling at my raised voice.

"Maybe your daddy can beat up my daddy," she says. "Maybe not. Who knows? But I've already put your mummy to sleep and I'm about to step into her somewhat cheap-looking shoes."

"Or not," I say. At first, I was too freaked out to think straight. Now I'm thinking straight. I give my backpack a sudden kick. It starts to shift and squirm. The flap opens and the marbles come shooting out. They form into the shape of an arrow and hurtle straight at Vanessa.

I scurry behind the couch and peer over the top. She

takes a few steps backward, reaches down into one of Irina's black boots, and pulls out a gun. She swings her arm around and starts blasting.

The room is filled with explosions of powdered glass. Vanessa doesn't even break a sweat. She methodically fires at each of the marbles, hitting her target every time. I watch in horror and mounting sadness as I see these little glass heroes that served valiantly by my side, that kept me alive all day, shatter under her relentless barrage of bullets. It seems to last for hours but it's probably more like seconds. Finally, the last of my marbles is a pile of fragments on the floor.

Vanessa grins at me as I cower behind the couch. "I think you've lost your marbles," she says, savoring every syllable.

I hate her. I hated her when she was Blabby. I hate her more now that I know who she really is, but most of all I hate her for what she just did. I charge out from behind the couch and rush at her. I don't even think about what I'm doing. I just know that anger of a sort I've never felt before is coursing through me.

"Really, peanut?" mocks Vanessa, pointing her gun straight at me. I stop running and push a hand into my pocket, where I feel something soft and squishy. The magnetic chewing gum Irina slipped into my pocket as I boarded the elevator in the Dominion Brothers Building. I yank it out and throw it up at the ceiling. It sticks.

"I think you might show a little respect for other people's property," she smirks.

She stops smirking as the gun flies out of her hand and hits the ceiling barrel-first. Vanessa's air of calm condescension deserts her. She stares up at the ceiling and then back at me. Then the syringe is pulled from her hand and speeds upward, leaving Vanessa jumping up in the air trying to grab it.

While she flails around, I do a backward somersault onto the couch—yes, even without the aid of nanosneakers, I'm still capable of a half-decent somersault. I land on a pile of cushions. I let myself sink down and then, with all the strength I can muster, I jump as high as I can go. I hurtle over Vanessa's grasping hands, grab the gun and syringe from the ceiling, and land on the ground with a stumble.

"Like a graceful young swan," she scowls.

Clearly, I got to her. I shook her unshakable air of superiority. I'm the part of her plan she didn't plan on, if that makes any sense.

"You're not going to shoot me," she says.

"You don't know that," I say, feeling cool and in control.

"I fired every bullet," Vanessa points out. I see her confidence returning. She's so sure of herself she doesn't even bother lying.

"I can still put you to sleep," I say, brandishing the syringe.

"But you won't." Vanessa almost yawns. "Because you'd never find out the answer to the multiple choice question."

"What multiple choice question?" I ask, and immediately wish I hadn't.

Vanessa holds up a finger indicating her desire for me to wait in silence for her next move. She's so irritating. I can't stand her. She reaches behind her to the bookcase, picks up her phone, and tosses it to me. I try to catch it while holding on to the gun and the syringe. The phone hits me in the chest but I bring my face down and catch it under my chin. Lightning-fast spy reflexes still intact. I sink toward the ground, put the gun on the floor, and then let the phone fall into my free hand.

"Click it on, there's a dear," says Vanessa.

I do, and Ryan's face fills the screen. His eyes are closed and his mouth hangs open.

"Ryan Wilder: A) sleeping, B) drugged, or C) dead?" asks Vanessa. "These are your choices. Put the syringe down and you may find out."

Ryan! My rage is mixed with a sudden burst of guilt. I never gave him a single thought. All that time they spent together and I never once worried about what she might have done to him.

"I know, peanut," says Vanessa, giving me that pout of fake sympathy. "I think three steps ahead, too. It's in the Dominion DNA."

"Where is he?" I shout at her. "Did you hurt him?"

"Where's my sympathy?" she asks, widening her eyes and acting like she's offended. "I had to spend weeks with him. No easy task, let me tell you. Laughing at his jokes, listening to him plan his next incredible prank, kissing him. . . . Well, actually, that part wasn't such a chore. Nice full lips."

Ew, ew, ew! Be ice, Bridget. Be stone. Don't give her the satisfaction of letting her see she's getting to you.

Vanessa gives me a nasty little wink. I let out a shriek of rage and throw the syringe straight at her. She doesn't flinch. As the needle flies, she spins around with a balletic grace that fills me with envy. Vanessa extends a long leg and kicks the needle straight back at me.

I let out a yelp of fright, grab a pillow, and hold it out in front of me like a dartboard. The syringe sinks into the middle of the cushion. I toss it aside and look for a suitable weapon. My eye falls on the iron candlesticks.

"So we're going to do this?" says Vanessa.

She's standing by the fireplace, pulling out big, thick pieces of chopped wood.

"It's getting done," I snarl, and I try to lift the nearest candlestick off the ground. It weighs a ton. I can't budge it.

Vanessa pivots and comes running at me, massive chunks of wood in either hand.

I seize two cushions from the couch and throw them at her. They sail straight past her head.

"Nice try," she laughs.

Vanessa starts swinging her pieces of wood like they're ax handles. She's close enough that I feel the wind on my face. I retreat to my familiar hiding place behind the couch, but as I sink to the ground I kick out my feet and shove the couch toward her. I hear an *oof* of surprise as her knees make contact with the couch and she falls forward. As she does, I leap up and run out the living room door. A second later, I hear her footsteps hit the wooden floorboards of the hallway.

"I'm disappointed, peanut," she calls after me. "Your brother didn't put up a fight. I expected more from you."

I grab the nearest vase of flowers and throw it at her. Never taking her mocking eyes off me, Vanessa calmly sidesteps the vase and smiles as it shatters behind her.

"You know, I'm actually glad things worked out this way," she says. "I don't particularly approve of guns. They're too easy. They keep you from developing other skills."

Vanessa reaches down to the bamboo umbrella stand and takes out a rolled black umbrella with a hook handle. A lone green umbrella remains in the stand. Vanessa sees me gazing at it. She takes a step backward.

"Go ahead," she says. "Let's do this as equals."

I reach out for the green umbrella. Vanessa lunges forward, wielding her umbrella like a sword. I whip a hand out and grab a picture from the wall. The sharp point of the umbrella smashes the glass of the photo. For a second, she keeps pushing the point of the umbrella into the frame, shoving it into my chest. The more pressure she applies, the more likely the point of the umbrella is going to break through the wood and stab straight into me. In desperation, I kick my leg up and knock the umbrella out of her hand. We both watch as it sails into the air. I jump first and grab it. As I come down, I see Vanessa snatch the green umbrella from the holder. This time my landing *is* like a graceful young swan.

"Impressive, peanut," she says, giving me a nod of respect. "Maybe we are equals, after all."

She steps into her sword-fighting stance, extending

her left arm, holding the green umbrella out at me with her right hand. She slowly brings her right knee forward.

Feeling self-conscious, I do the same. In one sudden, fluid movement, Vanessa tosses her umbrella in the air and catches the pointed end. She curls the hooked handle around my ankle and gives a sharp tug. My foot is yanked from under me. She kicks out at my other ankle and I lose my balance. As I flail midfall, Vanessa springs at me, pushing me down to the ground. Her knees dig into my thighs; the midsection of her umbrella presses heavy against my throat.

"This is a good lesson for you," she grins down at me. "Never trust the enemy, especially when she leads you to believe you're her equal. Because peanut, you are far from my equal."

Vanessa pushes down hard on the umbrella. I can't breathe. I can't speak. I feel my eyes bulging out.

"Not the most triumphant day for the Wilder family," she says. "First Ryan, now you. I get the feeling lovely little Natalie would be a more worthy opponent."

As she talks, I grope blindly, hoping to find a weapon. My fingers make contact with something long and pointed. The end of the black umbrella. I barely have the strength to grasp the tip of the umbrella but I manage to swing it up at Vanessa and tap her on the shoulder. She looks up and I swing harder. This time the handle hits her right in the nose.

"Ow ow ow ow!" she howls, clasping both hands around her nose. I sit up and Vanessa falls backward, her head hitting the ground hard.

"Ow ow ow ow!" she howls again.

I scramble to my feet and flee to the kitchen. I slam the door closed and prop a chair against the handle. I lean forward, grip my hands against my knees, and try to calm down. My instinct is to get out of this ironically named safe house and run as far away as possible, but I can't leave Irina and I have to find out where Ryan is. I have no choice but to go back into the living room. Which means neutralizing and interrogating Vanessa. And I can do that. I am her equal. She had the element of surprise but I constantly outwitted, out-jumped, out-gadgeted and outfought her.

I stand up straight and my breathing returns to normal. I look around the kitchen for items I can use to defend myself should Vanessa instigate another battle. There's so much to choose from. There's an old kettle, a frying pan, a meat tenderizer, a pizza slicer, an apple corer, a tin tray with star-shaped cookie cutters. I pick up a spatula. I'm armed and dangerous.

Vanessa doesn't stand a chance.

I reach for the kitchen door and the handle explodes in

a shower of splintered wood. I scream and stagger backward. The chair falls forward and the door swings open. Vanessa stands in the doorway, the gun in her hand, her nose starting to turn purple.

"Remember the lesson about never trusting the enemy?" she says with what I have quickly come to recognize as Classic Vanessa Condescension. "That also applies when she tells you she fired every bullet."

There it is. That smug superiority. I throw the spatula straight at Vanessa's face. Without taking her eyes from mine, she lifts the gun and fires at the utensil.

Click.

This time she really is out of bullets. If there was ever an occasion to seize the moment, this is it. I go to grab the frying pan from the stove but Vanessa moves faster. She whips the metal pan from the burner and does one of her long graceful lunges straight at me. I see the pan fly at my face and I do one of my chaotic jumps, throwing myself out of the pan's path, and land on the kitchen table. I feel it sway under my weight.

Vanessa swings the pan at my ankles but I jump up and over it. As I land, one of the table legs snaps. I propel myself off the table just before it breaks and leap onto the top of the big red fridge and, from there, onto the shelves at the back of the kitchen. I cling to the top shelf with one hand and try to get a toehold on the middle shelf.

"You look like a monkey hanging up there, peanut," says Vanessa. "A dirty, smelly monkey."

"That's sweet, Blabby," I reply, and throw the contents of a glass sugar jar at her. She waves her frying pan at the oncoming cloud of sugar, but from her coughing and spluttering, it's clear some of the grains hit their target. Encouraged, I grab the next jar from the shelf and douse her with flour.

"Stop it," she squeals.

"Sure thing, honey," I say, and, of course, throw the honey jar at her. She waves her pan at the oncoming honey. Dumb move, Duchess of Cambridge. The pan smashes against the honey jar, causing the contents to land on her head.

"It's in my hair," she screeches, and drops the frying pan.

When I first met Vanessa Dominion in the dim distant past of twelve minutes ago, she was a vision of icy cool. Now, her nose is a deep shade of red, her shimmering blond hair is coated in honey, her chic black cocktail dress is covered in flour, and her enviable poise has entirely deserted her.

"Nobody beats me in the kitchen," I say, savoring every syllable. (It's a line from an old action movie my dad watches every time it's on cable, but I feel like I just made it my own.)

I know what I have to do now. I have to overpower and subdue Vanessa. I have to tie her up and hide her away. Then I have to get Irina to safety and find Ryan. It would be a lot for a lesser spy, but I feel up to the challenge.

I leap—like a young gazelle rather than a dirty, smelly monkey—off the shelves and reach for the frying pan she foolishly discarded.

But as I hurtle toward Vanessa, she spins around, lashes out her leg, and kicks open the fridge door. It flies backward and hits me full in the face.

"Remember that time at your parents' house when you hit me with the fridge door?" Vanessa says as I fall. "This looks like it hurt quite a bit more," she says. "I certainly intended it to."

I see a blond blur above me. I can't focus on her face. I'm not sure where I am. I can't keep my eyes open.

"That's right, peanut," I hear an echoey voice say. "You go to sleep. It'll all be better in the morning. For me. When your mummy sees me take her crown. But for now, *oleya nagusu moomane . . .*"

Wait, what?

# CHAPTER TWENTY-FIVE

# Don't Leave Me Hanging

"Don't scream," says a voice. "Don't cry. Don't freak out. Listen to me. Focus on the sound of my voice. Open your eyes slowly."

Is that Ryan? It sounds like Ryan. But what would Ryan be doing here in the kitchen of the safe house? I attempt to open my left eye. It requires more effort than I imagined, and now that it's open, it hurts. A lot. I try to blink the water out of my eye so I can see straight but I feel like my head is swimming and there's a roaring in my ears. As I slowly regain consciousness, I become aware of an odor. It's a hot-garbage-on-a-humid-day kind of smell, and I feel like I'm going to gag.

"Are you okay?" Ryan's voice says.

"I don't know," I try to say. My mouth feels like it's filled with sawdust. My throat stings when I swallow.

"I need you to stay calm for me," Ryan says. "I know this looks bad but I'm going to get us out of here, I swear."

The uncharacteristic urgency in his voice blows away my cobwebs. I open both eyes and focus. Ryan's face is inches from mine. His hair is sticking straight up. Except it isn't . . .

Ryan is hanging upside down. His hands are tied behind his back. The rope binding his ankles together is suspended from a metal hook attached to a long silver rail filled with similar hooks. The other hooks have nothing hanging from them, but I'm guessing from the dried red blood splashed across the dirty white floor and the dirtier white walls, those hooks used to have things hanging from them. Now there's only Ryan and me, dangling in what I very much hope is a disused meat storage facility. Even though there are no cow carcasses here, the odor of meats past hangs in the air. Once again, my throat constricts. I feel like I'm going to throw up, but if I do, I'm going to be sick down my own face. The thought of that makes me feel even more sick. And then I think about who put me here.

Vanessa.

I don't feel any less sick, but now it's accompanied by a burning rage. She did this to Ryan. What's she done to Irina? Where's Strike?

What did she say to me before I blacked out?

"How long have we been here?" I ask Ryan.

"I don't know," he says. "You were still out when I woke up. Are you hurt? Did you see who brought you here? Have you seen Abby?"

Ryan's voice is getting shaky. He starts trying to squirm his way out of the ropes that hold him. I watch his face redden as he swings back and forth on the hook like the hand of an old grandfather clock.

"Ryan, take it easy," I say.

"She must be so scared," he says. "How could I let this happen?"

"It's not your fault," I say. Just when I thought it was not possible to hate Vanessa Dominion any more than I already do, she ascends to a new level of evil. Vanessa knew exactly what she was doing by locking me in a room with Ryan.

"She doesn't see the world like we do," Ryan moans. "She's so trusting, so childlike."

"Huh?" I say.

"I know you never liked her. All the times she tried to

reach out to you and you threw it back in her face. Why doesn't Bridget like me? That's what she used to say to me, and she always had tears in her eyes when she said it. And now she's gone. She could be anywhere. She could be . . ."

He can't finish his sentence and I can't make him feel worse by doing it for him.

Ryan strains against the ropes knotted around his wrists and ankles. He keeps moving from side to side, trying to make the rope fray against the hook. What should I do here? Do I tell him the truth about Vanessa? He's only just discovered he has a heart. I can't break it already. But if I don't tell him, he'll be driven mad by the sudden inexplicable disappearance of his girlfriend.

I have to choose how deeply I want to scar my brother.

Well played, Vanessa.

"Ryan, stop wriggling on the hook like a worm," I say.

"Start wriggling," he shouts at me. "Do something. We've got to get out of here and find Abby."

"That's what I want, too," I say, and I'm not lying. "But let's think this through logically. Where were you when she vanished? What's the last thing you remember?"

The wriggling ceases.

"Abby wanted to go to Chinatown," he says. "She

was on the platform. I jumped the turnstiles because the train was about to leave. The subway ticket guy shouted after me that I was in big trouble. When we got to our station and we were out in the street, I lost Abby in the crowds. I tried to run after her and then I don't know what happened; everything went black." Ryan goes silent for a second and then says, "I should have paid the fare. We could have caught another train. I put a target on both of our backs."

"You think the subway people are behind this?" I say. "Taking Abby, tracking me down, hanging us on hooks?"

"I'm not from here," he bawls. "I don't know how they do things."

Ryan goes back to swinging and wriggling. His exertions seem to make the knots tighter.

A sneaky thought pops into my head. "What if she's seeing someone else?" I say.

"What?" he groans.

"You're right, I don't care for Blabby, but we're just exploring possibilities here. What if she used the free trip to New York to hook up—no pun intended—with the other person she's seeing? Not that I'm saying there is one, but if there is, wouldn't that explain her random disappearance?"

"The pressure of blood on your upside-down brain

has made you go mental," says Ryan. "Not a word of what you just said was anywhere near sane."

"Maybe you're right," I say. "Because you know every little thing about Miss Abigail Rheinhardt. You know every little thing about who she knows, you know every member of her family and every one of her friends and you know for an absolute flying certainty she doesn't have a boyfriend in New York she never told you about. A boyfriend who would be capable of going to extreme lengths to get you and me, the little sister who never liked her, out of the way."

"That's crazy," says Ryan. But he says it quietly, as if he's thinking about it. And that's all I wanted to do. I just wanted to sow a few seeds of doubt and let Ryan's imagination bring forth a beautiful garden of paranoia and suspicion.

"I mean, how . . . ," I hear him say. "I mean, I'd know if . . ."

"'Cause it's not like people you meet online ever lie about themselves," I say, deliberately overdoing it. "Everyone online tells the absolute truth. No one has a hidden agenda. No one keeps secrets. No one's so blinded by someone they don't know claiming to like them that they believe everything that person says."

"Shut up," shouts Ryan. I know I've hit a nerve. I

know his fear is now tinged with speculation.

"But maybe I'm wrong," I say mildly.

"I would know if she was lying," he says. "Wouldn't I?"

We hang in silence from our respective hooks. Ryan's mind is, I imagine, swarming with the most horrifying thoughts. He's probably replaying his last few weeks with Abby/Blabby/Vanessa and starting to question everything he took for granted. He's probably feeling like the biggest sucker of all time. Good. That's how I want him to feel. Because the alternative—finding out he's the pawn of an ambitious criminal who drugged him, then hung him on a hook—is way worse. He'd never be able to trust anyone again. I know a little about how that feels. I don't recommend it.

"What about your secrets, Bridget?" Ryan suddenly says.

"My what now?" I squeak, taken aback.

"We never talked about where you went all those times you snuck out at night. Or how you suddenly developed this tough, confrontational personality. How'd all that happen, Bridget?"

Ah. I didn't want to tell Ryan the hideous truth about his appalling girlfriend, but should I tell him the exciting truth about me? We're stuck in this smelly white room hanging upside down from hooks. It's not like we have anything else to do. I take a second to decide the simplest way to explain it to him. I breathe in, which is a mistake because it's noxious.

"I—"

"Do you hear that?" Ryan hushes me with a gesture.

I listen. Footsteps and muffled voices, both of them getting louder. The sound of a thick metal chain being dragged from the handle of a door. The sound of a key in a lock.

"Oh God," says Ryan.

It's Vanessa. I know it's Vanessa. She's come to gloat, come to luxuriate in her superiority over me, come to crush what's left of Ryan's heart.

From my upside-down position, I see the metal door open. A cold wind rushes in and overpowers the smell.

"Nice to see you guys hanging out," says Joanna.

"Some people will do anything to avoid going to the Brooklyn Flea," says Sam Gunnery.

"Gunnery," I snarl. "I asked you to do one thing. When I get down from here, I'm kicking your butt."

"Fair enough," he says, unworried. "But maybe first you want to thank me and this little dude for tracking you down."

Sam squats and holds a closed fist inches from my upside-down face. He opens it to reveal a long-lost friend.

"Red!" I gasp. "Oh, Red, I thought I'd never see you again."

"Who's Red?" I hear Ryan say.

"The love of her life," Joanna says.

She starts to tug at Ryan's ropes, and as she does, she casually says, "So you know your sister's a spy, right?"

# CHAPTER TWENTY-SIX

# That Little Gang of Mine

"Bridget?" I hear Ryan call after me as I stumble out of the abandoned meat place into the chill of a New York Saturday morning.

"Is it true? What she's saying, is it for real?"

I know Ryan's having to process a lot of new disturbing information. For example: he doesn't really know his girlfriend. For another example: she might have used him to get to New York and then abandoned him on a crowded street. He has to consider Joanna's revelation that I am the offspring of two spies and still have ties to the family business.

"It's complicated," I tell him. "But yes, that's my secret and now it's yours." I scowl at Joanna and Sam. "Do a better job than those two," I say to Ryan. He looks shell-shocked and I don't blame him, but at least he's safe. Unfortunately that doesn't mean I don't have a lot to worry about. It's been hours since Vanessa showed me the literal door. She could be anywhere. Irina could be anywhere. Strike could be anywhere. What do I do? Who do I try to find first? Which birth parent can I actually save? I feel my teeth start to chatter and I realize I'm freezing. Vanessa did me the huge favor of removing my tourist garb, but all she left me was a white T-shirt and jeans.

And all of a sudden, I'm enveloped with warmth.

"Here," says Sam, and I realize he's given me his hoodie.

I shrug it off and kick it back at him. Not my smartest move because—I don't know if I mentioned—I'm freezing. But I'm also mad at him, and with good reason: he ran when he should have stayed and found Strike, and he betrayed a confidence. Sure, Joanna probably already knew I was a spy, but he never should have confirmed it. If I have to keep secrets, everybody has to keep secrets.

Sam bends down to pick up his hoodie. "I don't have cooties," he says.

"Beg to differ," I retort, and yes, I know I'm being harsh, but this kid has a way of getting under my skin.

He blinks at me. "I let you down," he says. "I freaked out. We're not all spies."

I feel myself soften toward him.

"And I came back for you," he says. "That's got to count for something."

"You came back . . ." I look at my watch. It's ten minutes before nine on Saturday morning. Last time I saw Gunnery it was late on Friday afternoon. "Fifteen hours later." It might even be more. Numbers are not my strong point.

"He tried to sell the marble to some dude he owes a ton of money," Joanna suddenly says.

"Shut up," Sam growls at Joanna.

"Username tedb," I say, giving Sam my best steely glare. "I remember."

His cheeks redden. "That's not what happened." He pauses and grimaces. "That's not all that happened. I was going to use Red to settle the debt . . ."

"Who's Red?" I hear Ryan ask.

"But when tedb said yes, I switched Red for a double. I was always going to bring the real Red back."

Sam looks to Joanna for confirmation. She nods. "He went back to the Forties looking for you. Then he came to Brooklyn. He spent the night on his police scanners and calling all his shady underworld contacts. He even concocted a crazy story for Alex that you'd been stopped in the street by a casting director for some indie movie about homeless clog dancers."

"Your story, if she asks, is that your one scene took all night to shoot and you were so convincing they expanded your role," says Sam. "You're Roxy, the one-legged clogger who isn't letting her handicap stand in the way of her dream."

I find myself laughing for the first time in what seems like a long time.

"We got out of Brooklyn Flea duties by telling Alex we'd both been cast," says Joanna. "I'm K-Clog, the reigning champion who knows her time is up but wants one last shot at homeless clogging glory."

Sam says, "I'm Buzz, the cynical con man who discovers Roxy clogging at the bus station and decides to do something good with his life."

"I love this movie," I say, because I do. I really want to see it. I take the hoodie from Sam and nod my thanks.

"Sorry it took so long to track you down," he says. "I'm in the favor business. I don't want anyone hating me."

"Stop saying things like I'm in the favor business and they won't," I say.

Sam nods and gives me a tentative *so we're good?* smile.

I put the hoodie on and start to struggle with the zipper. Sam goes to help me but Joanna elbows him out of the way.

"Move, doofus," she says to him. Joanna has even more trouble getting the zipper to close than I did. As she tugs at it, she lowers her voice and says, "Sam's not the worst person in the entire world."

My recent acquaintanceship with Vanessa Dominion leads me to agree with that.

"He did me a favor," she continues. "Alex didn't want to take me in at first. She'd never admit it, but it's true. Sam totally sold me to his mom. He made me sound like a shining angel from heaven. And it wasn't because we're such a close family. I know he did it so it would take the spotlight away from all the shady deals he does, but still . . ."

Joanna has this wistful little smile on her face. It's unsettling.

"So you're telling me he's selfish and he has secret agendas?" I say.

"I'm telling you things worked out for me because of him," she says, yanking at my zipper. "He's a good person to have on your side."

Ryan pushes Joanna away from the hoodie. He pulls

the zipper up to my neck with one quick movement.

"I'm probably not a good person to have on your side," he says. "But my girlfriend disappeared, I got hung on a hook in a meat locker, and my sister's a spy on a secret mission. Something's going on and I want in."

"You don't," I tell him. "You really, really don't."

"I want in, too," says Sam.

"I don't want in at all," says Joanna, scowling. "But it looks like that's the only way I get to hang out with you."

I am almost touched by Joanna's lovely sentiment, except for the huge amount of resentment in her voice.

"So what's the mission?" says Ryan, rubbing his hands and looking way too excited.

**We leave the** stench of dead animals and head to a half-empty diner on Mott Street, just north of Canal Street. I rip through a plate of buttered pineapple bun and eggs in under a second, such is my extreme hunger. I'm now attacking a fried fish ball and sausages. As I chew, swallow, and gurgle down a passion fruit green tea, I explain the situation to my three companions. I mean, at this stage, why not? Joanna and Sam know about the Forties. Sam saw the man in the Strike mask. Who am I protecting? I obviously do not reveal to Ryan that Blabby = Vanessa, but other than that small, trivial detail, I tell my brother, my friend, and Sam Gunnery that Strike and Irina are missing and that Edward Dominion's lethally psychotic daughter plans on carrying out my biological mother's final assassination. I conclude with the small but important detail that I do not, as yet, know the target of Vanessa's bullets.

When my summation of my last twenty-four hours in New York is complete, I am met with three pairs of wide, staring eyes and three open mouths. Joanna's phone vibrates, breaking the silence. She picks it up and gives me a warning glance.

"Hello, Nancy Wilder, mother of Bridget and Ryan," she says. "Yes, they're right here."

Ryan looks stricken. "I lost my phone," he mouths to me.

"I lost mine, too," I mouth back.

"You know what, Nancy, they'd forget their heads if they weren't screwed on." Joanna is talking to my mom like they are old friends. I don't know how she picked up these social skills but I'm not complaining. "Cut the kids a little slack," she goes on, a friendly gurgling laugh giving her voice a melodic quality. "This town is a whirl-wind, so much to do and see. Their feet haven't touched the ground. Ryan's been hanging out with us, him and his interesting girlfriend . . ."

I look over at Ryan, who stares down into his squid dish.

"They all stayed over last night and they're still sound asleep. I'll have them both call you when they surface. Okay, great talking to you, Nancy, my love to Jeff and Natalie. You take care now. Bye."

"Wow," I breathe. "You said more words to my mom in the past thirty seconds than you did in the last seven years, and none of those words were bitter or resentful. You sounded like you actually cared."

"Neat trick," Joanna says. "I learned from the best." She inclines her head toward Sam, who is texting furiously on his phone.

Without looking up, he says, "Okay, I'm getting you both untraceable prepaid phones so that doesn't happen again. I'm uploading surveillance footage from the time Bridget and Irina climbed out the window of the Forties. I'm looking for film from Chinatown at around the time Ryan emerged from the subway. What else can I do? How else can I help?"

Three pairs of wide, staring eyes—one of them mine—and three open mouths—again, one mine—are trained on Sam Gunnery.

"Sorry, who are you again?" says Ryan.

"He's my cousin Sam," says Joanna.

"He might not have cooties," I say.

That cool, cocky, calculating quality I found so off-putting about Sam seems to have vanished. He owns that he did the wrong thing yesterday and he's making a conscious effort to redress the balance. Of course, knowing what I know of him, he's also doing it because I will now owe him a colossal favor.

"What happens if we get this footage?" says Ryan.

"When," emphasizes Sam. "My most reliable guy's on it."

"The Squirrel," I tell Ryan.

"Okay, what then?" says Ryan. "What's the plan?"

I take a mouthful of fish ball, and between chews, I say, "I want to save Strike but he doesn't need me. Yes, I left him in the direst situation imaginable, but that's been the case his entire life. We could race all over the city looking for him, but he'll find a way to survive. Vanessa's a huge narcissist. She'll keep Irina alive so she can say"—I adopt a cold, heartless British accent—"'Look at me, Irina. Watch me take your crown. Look at me, daddy. . . .'" I wait for the table to burst into applause at my acting abilities. There is no clapping, so I press on. "So we have to find out what Irina's last mission was and stop Vanessa from carrying it out."

"Is that all?" says Ryan. "I was worried we wouldn't

have time to go to the Central Park Zoo."

"You're not stealing a reptile," I warn him.

"I can maybe get a list of the most popular assassination targets," says Sam.

"Where would you get that?" says Ryan, who seems a little bit irritated whenever Sam opens his mouth. I can't say I don't understand.

"Deep web," says Sam.

"Right." Ryan nods then looks at me and mouths, "Deep web?"

Sam's fingers fly across his phone. As he texts, he says, "Did anyone—Edward, Irina, or Vanessa—say anything that would give you *any* kind of clue as to what this last job was about?"

All right, Bridget Wilder, so-called spy, do that thing where you retreat into your mind and play back every single event of the last day. Concentrate on the small details. The way Edward was sitting. The weapons Irina threw into her black bag. Vanessa's face when she walked away from Irina's body. Was there something I missed? An overheard conversation. A text I shouldn't have seen. Anything?

Something bubbles to the surface. Something Vanessa said to me after she hit me with the fridge door. I was losing consciousness. Nothing made sense at that point. One minute she was talking in her precise, cut-glass

English accent. The next she was speaking gibberish. She said something like . . .

"Oh-ley-ah. Na-ga-su. Moo-manay," I say, tentatively sounding out the words I think I remember hearing her utter as I blacked out.

The other three give me baffled, slightly concerned looks.

"She invented a private language for us to communicate in, when we were like seven or eight," Joanna tells Sam. "She was weird even then." Joanna leans toward me. "Is that what you're doing now? Speaking in a private spy language you just invented?"

"No." I can't believe she brought up the long-repressed memory of Bridgannese, the secret vocabulary that would have made us seem fascinating to other people if Joanna had bothered to learn even a few words from the Bridgannese dictionary I made for her.

"I remember that!" hoots Ryan. "She used to have . . . remember, you had that sign, Bridget's Room: Keep Out, on your door, and then one day, it had changed to this insane mixture of symbols, numbers, and letters."

"It would have made sense if you'd read the dictionary," I say, reddening.

Joanna and Ryan are both laughing too loud and too long.

Sam grins at me. Great. What's he have to say?

"I used to do things like that," he says. "I remember when I was that age I drew a logo on my notebook. It said Gunnery City in big, bold writing. I didn't even know what it meant but I liked the way it looked. I even got this kid who owed me a favor to get it printed on a T-shirt. Pretty soon, everyone in school wanted one."

"So basically your story's nothing like mine," I say. "Except to let me know you've always been cool."

"Well, you're cool now," Sam says.

Oh. That was nice. And unexpected.

"So that thing you were saying?" he goes on.

"That thing?" Right. The important mission. "This thing I think I remember Vanessa saying. I might be wrong, but it sounded like oh-ley-ah na-ga-su moo-manay."

Sam holds his phone up to my face. There's a microphone app on the screen. "Say it again, slow and clear."

I repeat the words I may or may not have heard.

"Let's see if there's a translation that makes sense."

Sam replays the recording of me saying "Oh-ley-ah na-ga-su moo-manay." I cringe at the way I sound all shrill and breathless. It's like when you accidentally see your reflection in a window when you're not prepared. I look like that?

"That's Trezekhastani," says someone who's approaching our table.

I hear the voice, but I'm still shuddering at the thought of my squeaky tone.

"It means 'Say good-bye to the memories of your youth,'" says the voice as it gets closer to us.

I see Sam glance up. He seems momentarily surprised, and then he smiles. "The Squirrel knows everything," he says.

"Not everything, apparently," says the owner of the voice.

I'm not thinking about how squeaky I sound anymore. I'm thinking that I know who's talking. I'm thinking that my heart is banging its way out of my chest. I look up to see someone I didn't think I was going to see again.

Dale Tookey.

# CHAPTER TWENTY-SEVEN

# Secret Squirrel

"Hi," I say, or rather squeak, as I gaze up at the boy standing a foot from our table holding a white plastic bag and confirm that, yes, this is Dale Tookey. Hacker for hire, double agent, someone I kissed twice and never heard from again: Dale Tookey is all those things. But what is he doing here?

"Hi," says Dale Tookey. His voice also comes out a little higher than he probably wanted. He looks legitimately stunned to see me. Sam gets up, takes the plastic bag from Dale, reaches inside, and hands two prepaid phones to Ryan and me. Sam pulls an empty chair from a nearby table and motions for Dale to sit down.

"Hacker," says Sam to the rest of us, by way of explanation. "He's a superhero in his own universe, but around flesh-and-blood, non-digital life forms he gets a little squirrelly, hence the name."

Dale doesn't smile. He darts sidelong looks at me and swallows hard.

"You're that guy," Joanna suddenly says. "Bridget, he's that guy. Your guy, you know, from that time . . ."

She beams at me and points at Dale like I don't know who he is.

"Hold up," says Sam, looking from Dale to me and back, his confusion evident. "You two know each other?"

"Of course they do," Joanna trumpets. "They're both spi . . ."

I see the small burst of panic on Dale's face. Suddenly, I get it. He's undercover.

I grab what's left of my fried fish ball and ram it in Joanna's mouth.

"Bwwiwww!" Joanna tries to shout.

Sam stares at me and then at Dale. I didn't really help the situation there.

"You're both . . . ?" Sam says.

"Spi . . . der . . . ," I start.

"Lovers," Dale completes.

"Spider lovers," I say. "Lovers of spiders."

"When did you ever love spiders?" says Ryan.

"Oh my God, you know nothing about me," I snap. "Spiders are my passion. I spend all my free time on spider websites like . . . like . . ."

"The web dot com," says Dale, giving me a *that's the best I could do* shrug.

"That's where we met," I tell Sam. "I was a big fan of the . . . of the . . ."

"Green jumping spider from Australia," says Dale. "And she wanted to know about the Goliath bird-eating spider indigenous to South America."

"Yeah, I'm over that one," I say. "I thought he was cool, but he's a self-obsessed spider who doesn't care about anyone else's feelings."

"You don't know the Goliath as well as you think," Dale says. "He likes hanging out with certain other breeds of spiders and he wishes he could do that all the time, but he's got a whole other life it's best you know nothing about. When you think he's ignoring you, he's actually protecting you."

"If the Goliath spider knew anything about . . . the people who study him, he'd know we don't need protecting, we just need a little acknowledgment that we exist."

"The Goliath spider knows the people who study him exist," says Dale.

"Well, if he knows, then . . ." I stop talking. He hasn't forgotten me. He's here doing a job. I need to respect that.

Joanna swallows the fish ball and glares at me. "Stop doing that. I could choke to death."

"We're talking about our mutual love of spiders," I say to Joanna, staring straight into her eyes. "That's how I know the Squirrel. That's the only way I know him."

Joanna nods and then, right in front of me, she mouths "It's not" to Ryan.

Sam is focused on his phone. He looks up at Dale. "Okay, I got the files you sent. I know too much human interaction makes you break out in hives, so I'll let you bounce out of here. I'll text you if I need anything else."

I don't see Dale for months and now he's going to disappear again? After two minutes. Just like that?

"Um . . . can I talk to the Squirrel for a second?" I say. I stand up and head out of the diner. "It's spider talk, you wouldn't be interested. I'll just be a minute."

I motion for Dale to follow me. Sam, Joanna, and Ryan all watch us shuffle out of the diner.

We walk in silence past a fish stall. I turn to him. "Listen," I say.

"Not here," he says.

Dale picks up his pace. I follow him to the corner of Mott Street, where the traffic is at its busiest and loudest.

"In case anyone's listening," he says.

I nod.

"I didn't know it was you," he says. "I don't ask questions. Sam wants something, I try to get it."

"What are you doing here?" I say, attempting to make myself heard over the roar of cars, buses, and garbage trucks.

"What are *you* doing here?" he asks.

The Saturday morning traffic is so loud, I have to shift closer to Dale, close enough that I need to hold on to his arms for balance, so close I have to lean in and whisper in his ear. I tell him about Strike's van, about the Forties, about Irina, and about Vanessa's plan. I finish talking and stay in the same position, my mouth close to his ear, my hands on his arms.

I had to travel three thousand miles, get attacked by Tasers, menaced by bikers, hit by a door, and hung on a hook but I've got that feeling again. The I-hate-to-say-it-but-I'm-going-to-say-it squishy feeling I had the first time Dale Tookey smiled at me. The same feeling I had when . . .

"Did you say Trezekhastani?" I yell in his ear. He jumps in fright. I grip his upper arms.

He nods. "'Say good-bye to the memories of your youth.'"

"Sam's mom drove us from the airport. It took forever. She said it was because the kid of some high-up from the Trezekhastan government is having some sort of party."

Dale checks his phone. "'Nurik Tubaldina, Trezekhastan secretary of state, and his wife, Valla, American-raised daughter of Savlostavian parents, celebrate the passage into manhood of their son, Atom, at two o'clock in the Trezekhastan Orthodox Cathedral.'"

The dots start to connect. "Vanessa called herself a chameleon. She said she could change her look and her accent. Why would she learn Trezekhastani? What use would she have for it? Unless . . ."

I don't want to say the words.

He stares at me. "Trezekhastan and Savlostavia have been at war for decades. There's been a shaky cease-fire over the past few years . . ."

I hear Irina's words. *I don't eliminate children.*

"But the assassination of the son of the Trezekhastan secretary of state in a church full of Savolostavians would end that cease-fire big-time," I say.

*God, Irina,* I think. *Why did you have to get into this line of work?*

*God, Vanessa,* I think. *Why did this have to be the job you chose to get your daddy to notice you?*

"Call the cops," says Dale.

"The cops?" I repeat. The words feel alien in my mouth. Spies don't call cops.

"They've got the manpower," says Dale. "They can search every guest and every car. They can cover every inch of the cathedral."

"Yeah, but—" I start to say.

"This is big," says Dale. "This is starting-a-war big. Too big for you, even with Joanna and Ryan in tow."

"And Sam," I say.

"Nothing's too big for him," Dale says. "Or so he'd like to think."

"What? Is he in trouble?" I ask. "Is that your job here? Busting Sam Gunnery?"

"Nope. He's just the bottom step on the ladder I'm climbing. A multinational corporation hired me to test its security. I needed to establish myself as the new hacker on the block. I got Sam to find me a place to crash and an untraceable IP address. But that's small potatoes next to what you're wrapped up in. That's big potatoes. Call the cops, Bridget. The cops will get the FBI involved."

"Really?" I say. "That's what you think I should do? Is that what Strike would do?"

Dale takes both my hands. "We know that's not what Strike would do. But there's too many people involved.

Too much that could go wrong."

He hands me his phone.

"Hey, spider lovers!" shouts Ryan. "We doing this or what?"

I whirl around. Ryan, Joanna, and Sam are walking toward us.

"Yeah," calls out Joanna. "When do we start the stupid mission?"

"What's the deal with you and the Squirrel?" Sam yells. "Why are you standing so close to him?"

I turn back to Dale. "You can't get them involved," he says. "I can't believe you told them anything."

The look on his face. The phone in his hand. The voices of my brother, my best friend, and Sam Gunnery getting louder as they get nearer. I can be a good friend and sister or a good spy. I can't be both. They can't get involved in this.

"What are you going to do, Bridget?" says Dale. "Time's running out."

What am I going to do?

# CHAPTER TWENTY-EIGHT

# Do the Right Thing

I call the cops. Anonymously on my prepaid phone. I give the barest of bare details. I say the son of the Trezekhastan secretary of state's life may be in danger. I end the call but I keep talking. I report a missing person. Abigail Rheinhardt, sixteen years old, around five foot four, gray eyes, unique dress sense. I do this for Ryan's benefit and then I drop the phone into the sewer. Dale's paranoia is infectious.

"Out of my hands," I say to the others. "The ball's in the NYPD's court."

Ryan, Joanna, and Sam all look disappointed.

"This trip is turning into a compete washout," whines Ryan. "I get dumped, I don't get to stop an assassination. . . ."

"You did the right thing," says Dale.

Sam walks up to me and positions himself between me and Dale. "Are you warm enough in my hoodie? Do you need me to get you something else?"

"I'm toasty, thank you," I reply.

"Good," he says. But he doesn't move. He just keeps standing with his back to Dale.

"Okay," Dale finally says. "I should probably . . ."

"Get out of here and back to doing whatever weird illegal stuff you do," says Sam, a little curtly.

"Okay," says Dale, again. "See you in the spider-lover forums."

"Arachnophiles unite!" I say, and make a five-legged spider gesture with my wiggling fingers. Dale does the same, and then he walks away.

"It was nice of you to humor him," says Sam. "I don't know if he's ever spoken to an actual girl before."

"Next thing, he'll be kissing one," smirks Joanna, shooting a knowing look in my direction.

Sam takes my wrist in his hand and starts to pull me toward the nearest subway station. He turns to me and grins. "If Big Log hadn't fallen downstairs, we'd never have met," he says.

"Yes," I agree. "I'm also thankful for her near-death experience."

His hand tightens around my wrist. "You," he says, "are something else."

What's happening here?

**I must not** be the sharpest spy in the knife drawer, because it's not until we're sitting in the F train headed back to Brooklyn and Sam suddenly says, "So . . . do you have a boyfriend back home?" that alarm bells start clanging.

"Tons of them," I joke. "One for every day of the week. Two for weekends. There's never been a better time to be Bridget Wilder. The demand is staggering."

"Who else would say something unbalanced like that?" he says, his hand touching my wrist again. "You're different. That's why I like you."

Oh no. Oh no no no no no.

"IreallyhavetotalktoJoannarightnowit'sreallyimport- ant," I gasp, and scamper across the train to the seat beside Joanna.

"I think Sam likes me," I say through gritted teeth.

"This is a moving train," she announces. "If you want to be understood, you have to speak up."

"Sam," I say, a little louder. "I think he likes me."

"You think Sam likes you?" Joanna repeats at the top of her voice.

I look around the subway car to see if any passengers have food I can ram in her big mouth.

"I don't think so," she says. "He can do much better than you."

"I hope so," I say. "Because now I'm uncomfortable around him, plus I've known him for like five minutes."

"And you do not make a great first impression," Joanna reminds me.

"I know!"

"So you're still into that Dale guy?" she asks.

"I think I am."

Ryan slumps down in the seat opposite us. "That's great," he says. "I lose one girl, you get two guys. How is that fair?"

"I don't want two guys," I exclaim.

Sam comes over to sit next to Ryan. "Let's get our stories straight for *la madre*," he says. I feel a burst of gratitude toward Sam for deflecting the conversation away from his interest in me, and I throw myself into brainstorming titles for the homeless-clogging dance contest movie, which, even though it does not exist, has become my favorite film of the year.

"*Clog Up*," I suggest, brilliantly.

"*Woodfoot*," says Ryan.

"*K-Clog's Last Dance*," says Joanna, making it about her.

We discuss how we're going to maintain this incredible lie. "Won't Alex be Googling *homeless-clogging dance contest movie* every six seconds?" I say.

"If it comes to that, I can probably get the movie made," says Sam casually. I stare at him to see if he's joking. He is not joking. I am suddenly very confused. This guy I barely know who has decided he likes me has just said he can make my favorite movie, and he didn't even say it like he was trying to impress me. He simply doesn't think anything's beyond him. Which is in itself impressive. But I remember the knot in my stomach when I saw Dale. There's no knot with Sam. I'm not saying there's never going to be a knot, but the knot I have with Dale is the only knot I need in my life right now.

"Stop those two guys," screams a passenger. "They stole my phone!"

Two hulking teenage boys jump off the train as the doors open. I look out the window. Three uniformed cops are huddled on the platform, all deep in conversation. They don't even notice the two boys boarding the train on the opposite side. The passenger who was robbed rushes over to attract their attention. What do I do here? Nothing? Or something?

As the doors begin to close, I leap up from my seat and run out. I hear Sam and Joanna coming after me. "Go back to Brooklyn!" I shout at them. "I'll call you." I turn and hurl Red at the closing doors of the subway car the two teenagers have just ducked into. He wedges in between the two doors.

"Stand clear of the closing doors, please," the metallic subway announcement voice commands.

I shove my hands into the gap and try to pull the doors open. Two hands insert themselves above mine.

"I always knew I was your role model," says Ryan. "Are we going to steal the train?"

I laugh in relief that it's not Sam. Then I laugh again because Ryan, when he's not mourning the loss of Blabby, can be fun to be around.

"Stand clear of the closing doors, please," the metallic voice insists.

Ryan and I lever the doors apart. I spring inside and search the subway car. Right at the back end, I see the two hoodie dudes surround a lone female passenger, lost in the music in her headphones. One of them leans close to her. The other dips a hand inside her bag and starts to pull out a tablet.

"Go, Red," I say, and throw my last remaining marble

the length of the subway car. Red hits the hand of the dipper. The guy yells in pain and drops the tablet back inside the bag. The dipper tries to grab Red, but of course he's way too slow. The little marble flies inside the second guy's hood in the general direction of his mouth. A muffled howl of pain emerges. So does a fragment of tooth. The female passenger rushes away. The dipper starts to give chase. He loses his footing and falls onto his back. I walk up to the fallen criminal and slip a hand inside the pocket of his hoodie. I pull out the stolen phone.

"Thith ithn't over," I hear his partner say.

I turn around. The hood is down. The boy, who doesn't look any older than fifteen, is massaging his jaw.

"Lose a tooth?" I say sympathetically. "Maybe the tooth fairy'll leave you thomething nithe."

The kid lurches toward me, menace in his eyes.

I open my hand. Red bounces up onto my palm. The kid stops in his tracks.

"Or maybe you'll lose a few more if I ever see you on the train again."

I watch the kid trying to construct a threatening comeback. Luckily, the train comes to a halt and the two perps make their exit.

I turn and walk back to Ryan, holding my favorite marble between my thumb and forefinger.

"Say hello to Red."

"I want one," he says.

"That can never be allowed to happen."

"My sister's a spy," he says, and he actually looks proud.

"Not a good spy," I say. "I let myself be talked out of my mission. I'm walking away when I shouldn't."

Ryan stands in the middle of the subway car, hanging on to the silver pole with one hand, swinging in a semicircle. "Listen," he says. "Nancy Wilder, aka our mom, walked out of a secure job to start her own courier business. Jeff Wilder is completely unqualified to shop in a Pottery Barn, yet he manages one. My record speaks for itself. I don't deliberately go out of my way to cause trouble. I just see the rules other people live by and I don't believe they apply to me. My point is, we're Wilders. We go our own way. We don't do what we're supposed to do. We do what we feel like doing. We may not always get it right, but when we make mistakes, they're our mistakes."

He continues swinging.

"Cool speech, bro," I say quietly. That actually might be the most Ryan's ever said to me in one spurt and it was worth the wait.

"I didn't mention Natalie because then the whole

Wilders-live-by-their-own-rules thing sort of falls apart," he says.

"I figured," I reply.

The train comes to a halt.

"We're going back, right?" says Ryan, with way too much enthusiasm. "We're going to stop the assassination."

"I'm going to try and sneak into the ceremony and make sure the police don't miss vital clues," I tell him. "You have all of New York to explore."

"Seriously?" he says, his face falling.

"You got hung on a hook," I tell him. "That's an awesome vacation story."

"Fine," he sighs.

I get off the train. Ryan stays. As I go, he yells, "Good luck with the spying."

I act like I don't hear him and hurry up the subway steps. I stop thinking about Ryan and start worrying about how I'm actually going to get into the cathedral now that I've alerted the city's police department to a possible attempt on the life of a prominent foreign politician's son.

Once I'm out in the street, I duck into a sneaker store and consider my next move. I wish I could talk it over with Dale Tookey, but he was the one who filled me with doubt. I can't call Dale now and tell him I'm going to back to the scene of the potential crime.

I take out my phone—oh wait, it's not my phone, it's the one I retrieved from the two hoodie dudes on the train; I brilliantly forgot to return it to its owner. Oops. I use this borrowed phone to make another call. I need to talk to someone I really do not want to owe a favor.

"Hi, Joanna? Can you put Sam on?"

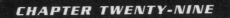

# CHAPTER TWENTY-NINE

# I Am Zamira Kamirov

"I am Zamira Kamirov."

"My name is Zamira Kamirov."

"Zamira Kamirov. My parents follow soon. I take my seat now, yes?"

I am in Alex Gunnery's bedroom, gazing at my reflection in her mirror and practicing my Trezekhastan enunciation for the biggest and most important lie I will ever tell.

Sam, credit where credit's due, came through 199.9 percent. I called him up, told him I needed to get into the coming-of-age celebration despite it being covered in cops. He told me to meet him back in his Brooklyn home, by which time he would have come up with a solution.

By the time Ryan and I reached his mom's brownstone, Alex and Lucien were already out spending their Saturday at the much-discussed Brooklyn Flea and Sam had proved as good as his word.

Sam, or someone who owed him a favor, had located the guest list for the celebration. Someone else coordinated the guests with the flight logs of the planes coming in from Trezekhastan and Savlostavia. Almost all the guests had arrived in the city the previous night. A handful were running late. Among that handful was Zamira Kamirov, teenage daughter of Trezekhastan's junior minister of agriculture, attending in place of her father, who was stuck at an international grain conference. Zamira Kamirov's Instagram account was not difficult to find. She's taller than me, but we both have short darkish hair, we both have the same kind of figure, and our faces are similar shapes.

"I can be her," I told myself. Except that all I have to wear is Sam's hoodie, a white T-shirt, jeans, and sneakers, none of which qualify as desirable celebration attire. So I improvised. I borrowed a black tuxedo jacket from Sam's closet, one of Alex's short skirts, which comes down past my knees, a pair of dark glasses that covers half my face, a hockey puck–shaped hat with a veil, and a pair of shoes that are two sizes too big for me but which I stuffed with balled-up toilet paper.

"Perfect," says Sam. "Wear that on our date."

Ah. Right. The other thing.

In order for Sam to do me this huge, possibly war-averting favor, I had to agree to go out on a date with him before I go back to Reindeer Crescent. Lives are at stake. Two countries hang in the balance. How could I say no? (Honestly? I had to think about it. Sam's a very, very smart, good-looking, insanely connected, scarily ambitious guy. If Dale Tookey hadn't resurfaced . . . no, even if Dale Tookey hadn't resurfaced, the kind of life Sam's leading is going to land him in horrific trouble somewhere down the line. Or it's going to make him a future president. Either way, I don't want to get involved beyond the one date I've committed to. Plus, still no knot.)

"I am Zamira Kamirov," I intone with confidence as I glide into the Gunnery kitchen, where Ryan and Joanna are gorging on sandwiches and chips.

I wait for their reactions.

"Huge improvement," says Ryan.

"Always wear that veil," says Joanna, and they cackle in unison.

"Ignore them," says Sam, joining me in the kitchen

and now, I can't fail to notice, wearing a black tuxedo. He reaches up to adjust my hat. "You look amazing."

"Um, thanks," I say, taking careful steps away from him in my too-big shoes.

Ryan crumples up his chip bag and throws it at the recycling bin, missing it by several inches.

He claps his hands. "Let's save the day."

"You're not saving anything," I say. "Joanna, babysit Ryan."

"But I'm coming with you," she starts to say.

"Ryan, babysit Joanna," I order. "Both of you stay here where it's safe. Monitor the police scanner on the computer. Let me know if anything suspicious happens outside the cathedral."

They both look let down.

"Oh, I'm so sorry you don't get to go to the most fashionable assassination in the city," I snap at them. "How can I be so mean and insensitive?"

"We never get to hang out," says Joanna. "You're only here till Monday."

I pull off my huge dark glasses, shove my veil on top of my hockey puck–shaped hat, and stare at her. "Now? You're accusing me of neglecting you now? We've talked every day since you moved here. You're happier than you've ever been."

"I have to work at it," she mumbles. "Being nice to people is hard. So is getting them to like me. I never had to work at it with you."

"Maybe you could try working at it a little bit with me," I say. "I'm here for two more fun-filled days. We've got time to hang out, just you and me."

I push my glasses back on. "Okay? Can I go now?" I pull my veil back down.

"Go," says Ryan, his mouth filled with the contents of a new bag of chips. "Enjoy."

"Later, y'all," says Sam, leaving the kitchen.

"How come he gets to go?" moans Ryan.

"Ask Bridget," he says.

"I . . . uh . . . need him," I say through gritted teeth.

"Oooh," Ryan and Joanna chorus. "Bridget needs Sam!"

And then they make stupid juvenile kissing noises and I'm relieved my glasses and veil prevent them from seeing my burning-red face.

# CHAPTER THIRTY

# Get Me to the Church on Time

"Check it out," says a guy named Footwear as he hands me a green passport. "Better than the real thing."

Sam and I are in the back office of an auto garage under the Brooklyn Bridge. The smell of motor oil is everywhere. Footwear, a large bald man wearing stained blue overalls with his name sewn into the chest, stands over me as I flip through the passport. The words are in Trezekhastani, but the picture is of me. Proof that I am, indeed, Zamira Kamirov.

"Nice work, Footwear," I tell him.

"Anything for my man here," Footwear says, punching Sam in the arm. "Never lets me down when I need Knicks tickets."

Sam tosses Footwear a friendly salute and guides me out of the office, through the garage, and onto the street, where the town car whose driver owed him a favor waits to open the door for us.

I climb into the backseat. Sam sits next to me.

"Okay, Reardon," says Sam to the driver. "The Trezekhastan Orthodox Cathedral."

"Corner of Twenty-Third Street and Eighth Avenue," says the driver. "Traffic's gonna be a challenge, but I'll get you there on time."

I check my watch. It's ten minutes after one. The coming-of-age ceremony is scheduled to start at two.

"You two make a cute couple," says Reardon the driver.

"She makes me look good," says Sam. He squeezes closer to me and whispers in my ear. "You know, your spy abilities. My people skills. We should team up. I'm not just talking about dating. I mean, we could really help each other out. We could trade information, dig up secrets for each other. You could help me look into people's backgrounds; I could help you gain access to pretty much anywhere you wanted to go. We could lock down both coasts."

And right there, in the tone of his voice, in the smooth way he lays out his vision of our joint future as if there's no doubt we're going to have one, I see how he gets what he wants. Sam's very persuasive, so much so that, when he was talking, I was thinking, *Why not? Sounds good. We could lock down both coasts. In fact, why stop at both coasts?*

The phone in my pocket rings. It distracts me from Sam's voice. I don't recognize the number on the screen, but then I remember this isn't my phone. It's the one I fished out of the pocket of the hoodie criminal who stole it on the subway.

"Hello?" I say.

"You have my phone," says a woman's nervous voice.

It's the hoodie guys' victim! I tell her how happy I am to hear from the owner of the phone I found quite by accident. I make arrangements to return it later this afternoon, and after the victim has thanked me profusely and hung up, I continue a one-sided conversation, pretending to tell my new friend all about my family, my school, and life in Reindeer Crescent. I maintain this charade for the entire thirty-eight minutes it takes Reardon to drive us into Manhattan because I don't want to give Sam any more opportunities to persuade me to team up with him and lock down both coasts.

At two o'clock, we're on Eighth Avenue and Seventeenth Street. The traffic ahead of us is not moving. The air is filled with angrily honking horns. I add to the noise by impatiently drumming my fingers off the window.

"If it's any consolation, everyone's in the same boat," says the driver. "No one's going to be on time today."

It's no consolation.

I go back to drumming on the window, and then I notice the limousine waiting in the lane next to us. A girl sitting in the backseat is staring blankly out of her window. She's looking in my direction. I recognize the boredom in her expression. I recognize something else. I know this girl from her Instagram account. I am this girl. Zamira Kamirov is in the next car.

She can't get to the cathedral at the same time as me. I squeeze past Sam and open the door nearest the curb.

"What are you doing?" Sam says. "Get back in."

"I need to buy some breath mints," I lie, and jump out of the car. "I'll be back in a minute."

"No you won't," he says, and starts to follow me out into the street.

"Sam, you've done a lot for me today, and I'm grateful," I tell him. "But you can't help me anymore and I can't be responsible for you getting hurt."

"I won't get hurt," he says.

"Remember how you found me this morning?" I remind him. "All beaten-up and hanging from a hook?

Your mother already doesn't like me. Imagine what she'd think if I let something like that happen to you."

"Nothing . . . ," he starts to say.

"Enough!" I bark. "Do yourself a favor and get back in the car."

Sam flinches like I slapped him. He probably thinks I'm mean. Good. The meaner he believes me to be, the safer he'll stay. I start to run up Eighth Avenue. I manage maybe three steps in my heels before I lose my balance and have to grab the arm of a shocked stranger. The passerby shakes me off. I lean against a street lamp and pull off Alex Gunnery's too-big shoes. Then I start running again. On the crowded New York sidewalk, shoes in hand, my stupid veil pushed up over my hockey puck–shaped hat, zipping around pedestrians, shoving my way through groups of teens idly shuffling along, narrowly avoiding collisions with mothers pushing strollers, nearly charging head-on into fully grown adults immersed in their phones, and all the while checking the uneven ground beneath my bare feet for garbage, open manhole covers, and smelly things that I do not want to step in. This probably isn't a smart way to get to my destination unscathed.

On Eighth and Eighteenth, I see a boy tumble off his skateboard and roll onto the sidewalk. As he tries to sit upright, I jump onto his board, kick out with my left leg, and shoot up the street.

"Hey!" I hear him yell behind me.

"Sorry!" I call back.

With my veil flying and my shoes in my hand, I probably don't look a lot like the average skateboarder. The New Yorkers who scatter out of my way as I rocket along the sidewalk are shouting abuse and jabbing angry fingers at me. I know I'm a hazard but I can't help it. I'm in a hurry.

From halfway up Eighth and Twentieth, I can see the police presence outside the cathedral. The building is cordoned off with yellow tape. Limousines are lined up for inspection. Cops are checking inside the trunks, shining flashlights under the cars, and looking in the hoods. As I keep rolling, I see guests lining up in the street, each one being patted down by police officers.

I made this happen with one phone call, I realize. I also realize I'm a minute or so away from being patted down myself.

I slow down my pace as I approach the corner of Eighth and Twenty-Third. Police cars and local news trucks surround the cathedral. I hop off my stolen board, squeeze back into my shoes, wipe the thin film of sweat from my brow, and lower my veil.

"Celebration guests over here," yells a policewoman.

I join the end of a long, long line. Extravagantly dressed men, women, boys, and girls in front of me talk loudly and rapidly in languages that are either Trezekhastani or Savlostavian. I do not need a translator to explain that these people who have traveled long distances to attend this ceremony are not happy about waiting in the street to be patted down by American police officers.

The couple in front of me, a woman wearing a hat the size of a satellite dish and her rotund husband, both stop in the middle of their angry exchange and peer in my direction.

Uh-oh.

If they speak to me in either Trezekhastani or Savlostavian, I'm in trouble. If they know the real Zamira Kamirov—and the chances are fifty-fifty—I'm in huuuuge trouble.

Satellite Dish Hat starts yakking a mile a minute in what she must imagine is our shared tongue.

I remain silent behind my veil and dark glasses. Satellite Dish Hat doesn't give up. She leans toward me and speaks both louder and slower. Rotund Husband joins in.

How do I get out of this?

I burst into tears. Or at least, I shake my shoulders and make appropriately pathetic weeping noises.

"Saying good-bye to childhood is so-o-o-o sad," I manage to get out.

Satellite Dish Hat and her husband look embarrassed at my wailing. They turn around and resume their conversation. I sigh with relief but maintain my sniveling as a deterrent in case anyone else tries to engage me.

The police finally beckon to the couple in front of me. I watch as they hand over their passports and endure the rubber-gloved hands exploring their pockets for hidden weapons.

I turn around in time to see the real Zamira Kamirov take her place at the back of the line.

I feel my face go red and my heart start to thump. I whirl back around and watch Satellite Dish Hat and her husband receive the world's longest pat-down.

Hurry up.

Finally, the couple are escorted through the yellow tape and into a door around the back of the cathedral.

A police translator says something I imagine means "Step forward." I pass my forged Trezekhastan passport to the cop. He looks at the clipboard with the list of ceremony guests. Then he looks at me.

"You're here on your own?"

"My father at grain conference," I say. "My mother army tank commander."

The cop motions at me to lift my veil and take off my

dark glasses. He checks my passport picture.

Passing myself off as Zamira Kamirov is not my most fully thought-through plan. There is a large line of impatient guests behind me capable of outing me as an impostor. But luckily for me, it appears they have other things on their minds. Some of them are singing with passion and volume, a song that, even to my untrained ears, sounds like a national anthem. Behind them, a second group of guests has begun to try and drown them out by singing another anthemic song in a different language. The first group gets even louder. Together they sound like a choir of angry cats.

"Shut it down," roars the cop. "Shut it down right now or you're standing out here all day."

The cop pats my jacket pockets. He pulls out Red and gives him a suspicious stare.

"My lucky marble," I say.

The cop gives me a pitying look, drops Red into my hand, and then shoves my passport back at me before stomping off to deal with the dueling groups of anthem singers. Another cop guides me to the back of the cathedral. I hear organ music echoing from inside the building. I take a few more unsteady steps in my too-big shoes.

I'm in.

**CHAPTER THIRTY-ONE**

# Party Crasher

I'm seated eight rows from the front and six seats in. As I try to squeeze my way through the half-filled row without tumbling off Alex Gunnery's shoes, I feel eyes on me. Not from my fellow row mates; they couldn't be sweeter or more welcoming. No, these eyes are coming from the right-hand side of the cathedral. The Savlostavian side.

What the Trezekhastan Orthodox Cathedral lacks in grandeur—it can only seat about three hundred people— it makes up for in beauty. I'm stunned by the white marble floor, the artwork on the ceiling depicting a swirl of angels ascending to heaven, and the detail and crafts-manship of the stained-glass windows that surround me. But the atmosphere is heavy with pent-up hostility. The well-dressed occupants of the right-hand side are not happy to be here at this coming-of-age ritual. They are not happy to be so close, separated by only a single aisle, from their one-time enemies.

Every new addition to the left-hand side incites a mass of angry murmurs. I can't hear the words, and even if I could, I wouldn't understand them, but I can guess the meaning behind them. He's poor and common. Their child smells of lumpy milk. My companions in row eight are more sensitive to each new insult. Every time an usher deposits a fresh guest on the left-hand side, my row mates click their tongues, inhale sharply, and shake their heads with disapproval at the boorish behavior coming from the other side of the cathedral. I click, inhale, and shake along with them, but my attention is elsewhere.

I count four uniformed policemen in the cathedral. Two on either side of the door. Two at the bottom of the steps leading up to the altar. I see a man in an ill-fitting suit standing under a stained-glass window on the right-hand side of the cathedral. From the way his eyes continuously sweep the entirety of the room, I'm guess-ing he's a plainclothes cop. My eyes are also sweeping the entirety of the room. I'm looking for someone the size and shape of Vanessa Dominion. She may be bewigged, she may have a different posture and a different accent, but if she's here, I'm going to sniff her out.

I rise from my seat and gesture to my immediate neighbors to save my place. I totter out of the row and make my way up the aisle to the altar steps. I take out the phone I rescued from the subway hoodie guys and I brandish it at the cop standing closest to me.

"Is okay I make film for my muzzer and fazzer?" I ask, wildly overdoing my accent.

The cop gives me a suspicious look. I hand him the phone. "You don't trust me? You do it for me."

"Go ahead," the cop mutters. "But make it fast and then sit down."

I pretend to film the angelic vision on the ceiling but I'm really searching for a familiar face. I nod my thanks to the scowling cop and walk slowly back down the aisle, looking from left to right. I want to catch a glimpse of Vanessa, but more than that, I want her to catch a glimpse of me. I want her to feel nervous. I want her to be careless. I want her to remember that I was more than a match for her. I want her to remember that she told me her plans but I didn't tell her mine. I want her to be so rattled by the sight of me that she makes mistakes. I lift my veil and take off my glasses. Here I am.

"There she is!" screams an outraged, accented voice. "Liar! Impostor!"

The real Zamira Kamirov stands in the doorway of the cathedral with a group of New York cops grouped around her, an accusing finger pointed in my direction.

Uh-oh.

Do I run? Do I cry? Do I rely on Red? That's a lot of police officers for one small marble. I hear the footsteps of the cop stationed by the altar. Before he gets too close, I sprint over to the right-hand side of the cathedral. The Savlostavian side.

I look at the rows of disdainful faces, the big hats, the gold rings, the huge hoop earrings, the missing teeth, and I shout out two words. "Trezekhastan sucks!" I put on a terrified face. "They tell lies about me. They want to put me in their jail. I did nothing wrong."

The woman in the satellite dish hat purses her lips at me. "You sit on Trezekhastan side," she says, her eyes glittering with distrust.

"I didn't know," I wail. My accent is all over the map. I'm not sure whether I'm supposed to be American, Trezekhestani, or Savlostavian at this point. I'm drowning in a sea of my own lies! But I have to keep going. "I'm young and naive. I thought we could all be friends.

Now they call the cops on me."

Satellite Dish Hat beckons to me. "You sit with me," she says. "No one takes you anywhere."

"Thankyouthankyouthankyou," I babble, and squeeze my way next to the woman.

"Miss," calls the cop from the altar. "Come with me, please. You need to answer some questions."

Satellite Dish Hat waves him off. "She with us. Move on, Johnny Cop."

"I'm talking to the girl," he says.

I grab her arm. "Don't let them take me."

The woman spits out a short, angry sentence. Every man seated on the right-hand side of the cathedral rises to his feet. I'll say this about both sides. They may be mortal foes, but they've been very protective of me.

All the cops working in the cathedral come charging forward. The tension that's been building since I got here boils over. The Savlostavians throw their prayer books at the cops. The police officers start hauling guests out of the aisles and handcuffing them.

In the middle of the chaos, I get down on my hands and knees and crawl out of the row. I continue to crawl in the shadows under the stained-glass window. No one notices me. I keep shuffling along until I'm close to the cathedral doorway, where I see a stunned Zamira

Kamirov. I sympathize with her. She has to fly alone to a foreign country for a ceremony she probably doesn't care about. She gets stuck in a traffic jam and then reaches the cathedral only to be told someone with her name is already in attendance. And now the cops she hoped would right this wrong are fighting with the guests. Not a great way to spend your first day in New York, but guess what, Zamira, my first day wasn't much fun, either.

I jump to my feet, run toward the doorway, pull Red out of my pocket, and toss him in her direction. She opens her mouth to scream, giving him the perfect opportunity to jump inside.

"She's going to be fine," I tell the arriving guests who see the choking, red-faced girl flailing around in front of them. "Cough lozenge stuck in her throat. I'm taking care of it."

I grab Zamira by the arm and drag her to the ladies' room. She tries to struggle and pull away.

"Mmmm mmmm mmmm!" she protests.

I kick open the door and shove her inside.

"Mmmmm mmmm mmmmm!" she tries to scream.

I put my hands on her shoulders and look into her bugged-out eyes.

"Zamira," I say quietly and calmly, "I'm going to remove the marble from your mouth, but before I do, you have to promise not to scream, and you have to promise to listen to me. Do you promise?"

She stares at me like I'm a dangerous lunatic on the run from an asylum. I do not for one second blame her.

"Do you promise?" I repeat.

"Mmmm mmm." She nods.

I open my palm. Red jumps out of her mouth and into my hand. Ugh. Warm and wet. I drop him in my pocket and go over to the sink, where I squirt the contents of a little plastic soap dispenser onto my hand.

"Aaaaa . . . ," Zamira starts to scream. I clamp my soapy hand over her mouth.

The ladies' room door opens. I shove Zamira into the nearest toilet stall and kick the door shut behind me.

I touch my finger to her lips and nod at her. She nods back. I very slowly pull my hand away.

"Who are you?" she croaks.

"I'm a friend," I say. "Not a great friend, obviously. But I'm here to help stop a war between your country and Savlostavia."

"Those Savlostavian pigs," she says.

"Someone far, far worse is behind it," I tell her.

In a stall in the bathroom of the cathedral, I explain, in rapid whispers, to the daughter of Trezekhastan's junior minister of agriculture, that Vanessa Dominion is planning to shoot the secretary of state's son to impress her father.

"I understand if you don't believe me," I say at the end of my hurried explanation. "But I'm telling you the truth."

Zamira gives me a long stare filled with dislike. Once again, I don't blame her in the slightest.

"I'm the bad guy here," I tell her. "You want to scream, you want to have me arrested and thrown in jail, you have every right. I would if I were you. But there's something else you could do. You could let me be you. Tell the cops you're my stalker. Apologize and slip away."

"Then what I do?" she says.

"This is New York," I say. "Your trip had a bad start, but it doesn't have to carry on like that. I can help you have a better time, if you'd like."

"You get me ticket to *Spider-Man*?" she says.

"*Spider-Man* closed years ago," I say, and I empathize as her face clouds over with disappointment. "But if you want to see a show or get into a club or get a fake passport or have the best day in New York you've ever had, I can make that happen."

Her expression softens. I take out the phone and hit ten digits.

"Sam," I say. "I need another favor. I'm putting my

friend Zamira Kamirov on the phone. Whatever she asks, you say yes."

I hand her the phone. "Ask for the moon," I tell her. "He'll get it."

"And what about you?" Zamira says. "What are you going to do?"

"I'll tell you next time I see you," I say.

"We will meet again?" she says.

I shake my head. "No. Now go."

She nods and pushes past me. I watch the toilet stall door close as she leaves.

"This Sam?" I hear her voice start to fade. "I want to see sweaty men fight in a cage."

I take a moment to try and undo some of the damage crawling across the cathedral floor did to my fancy outfit. I smooth, tuck, and rebutton until I'm ready to return to my mission. I push open the stall door but I can't seem to get out. I feel something push back at me, but I don't see anything. I realize what it is—who it is—but I'm too late. I feel a sharp jab at the side of my neck. My vision blurs. My legs give way.

Vanessa stole more than a few teaspoons of the invisibility juice.

# CHAPTER THIRTY-TWO

# *Raging Waters*

It could have been a lot worse. I mean, my situation is not great. But I could have woken up to find myself buried alive in a coffin ten feet under the earth. I could be in a trunk in the back of a speeding car. I could be at the top of a bonfire with flames licking my feet. Compared to any of those situations, returning to consciousness and finding myself still in a bathroom stall and tied to the toilet is almost a relief. Almost. Thick, knotted ropes pull my arms back and tie them around the tank of the toilet. My legs are fastened against the bowl. I start to struggle and pull but it makes no difference. From outside, I hear the faint sound of swelling organ music and I understand why Vanessa didn't bury me, shove me in a trunk, or sit me at the top of a bonfire. She wants me to know I failed.

I try to call for help. That's when I realize there's tape over my mouth. I feel faint stirrings of panic. I can't move my arms and legs. I can't speak. There's nothing on the ground that might help me free myself. The ceiling is bare except for a light bulb hanging from a wire. Even though the stall is tiny, there's not enough room for me to bang my head off the walls. I'm out of options.

Except Red.

If I still have him. If she hasn't taken him. We've been together long enough for him to respond to my moods. *If you're still here, Red,* I think, *if you can understand what's happened to me, help me, get me out of this.*

I strain against the ropes and make the same sort of *mmmm* noises that came out of Zamira's mouth in this very same stall. It's not much, but it's the only way I know to communicate my need to be rescued. I strain and *mmmm* a little more.

Nothing.

The disappointment crushes me. I'm alone.

And then I feel a soft shuffling movement against my waist. I'm not alone.

Red bounces out of my jacket pocket and shoots into the air.

"Red!" I try to shout, but it comes out "Mmmmnnnggg."

The little red marble disappears over the top of the next stall. I hear a loud splash and then I hear nothing. This didn't have to happen. I didn't have to end up like this. I had options. Why did I have to be so stubborn? Why did I forbid Ryan, Joanna, and Sam from helping me? Why did I send Zamira away? Why didn't I listen to Dale and leave this in the hands of the cops? Why did I put all my trust in an unpredictable red marble? *If I ever get out of this toilet stall, I will be more of a team player,* I tell myself.

When did the rumbling start? Was it happening while I was bemoaning my lack of faith in others? I feel something moving. It's coming from directly underneath me. I feel the toilet seat start to vibrate. I hear a loud whistling noise. The toilet bowl is starting to shake. The whistling sound has altered in pitch and ferocity, sounding more like an endless hysterical scream. The toilet seat beneath me feels like a washing machine barely containing a full load. My own *mmmmmnnnnnggggggg*s match the noise from the bowl.

Oh my God.

I think I know what's happening down there.

I think Red's doing the same thing Ryan did a few years ago during his blowing-up-toilets phase, when he'd go to the house of a friend-slash-victim, unscrew the valve beneath the toilet bowl, and insert a golf ball into the water pipe. The pressure would make the bowl explode into a thousand pieces. Hilarious!

Except that I'm the one currently sitting on a toilet that is primed to explode.

The shaking is getting more violent. The screaming from the blocked pipe verges on the hysterical as my own *mmmmmnnnnngggggg*ing grows louder. I squeeze my eyes shut and start counting backward. Ten. Nine. Eight. Seven. Six. Five. Four. Three. Two. One . . . Zero. Zero minus one. Zero minus two. Zero minus . . .

*BOOM!*

A jet of water blasts the toilet up in the air. It's like being on a rollercoaster in that I feel like I'm about to be violently sick and I'm too terrified to scream. I look up and see the ceiling get closer. I hurl myself forward. The movement turns the toilet upside down so my head is now pointed toward the floor. The porcelain base smashes against the ceiling. The ropes fall from my arms and ankles. I am blasted full in the face by an explosion of dirty water that causes me to gasp and choke. I start to fall, but before I do, I wrap my ankles around the wire that holds a single light bulb.

For a second, I dangle, like a gasping, choking human bulb; then, as I feel the wire start to tear away from the roof, I swing myself from side to side until I've gathered enough momentum to let go. I fly through the door of the nearest stall, flailing wildly as I try to grab the door and make some kind of graceful landing. That doesn't happen. I hit the wall hard enough to knock the wind out of me and then I slide down the toilet bowl and land upside down on the wet ground. I lie in a breathless, trembling, sodden heap. Out of my one open eye, I see Red roll toward me. He stops a few inches from my face.

"Thanks," I try to say, but my mouth is still covered. I rip the tape off and reach to wrap my hand around the marble who broke me out of my prison.

"New York's kicked our butt since we got here," I say to him in a hoarse whisper. "Time we kicked back."

# CHAPTER THIRTY-THREE

# *Growing Pains*

From inside the cathedral, I hear a boy's high-pitched, trembling voice. I knock and kick at the doors. One door creaks open. An usher stares at me. When I first appeared at the ceremony, I was more than presentable in my all-black ensemble. Now I'm soaked in dirty toilet water and dripping all over the floor. Bits of porcelain cling to my hair. My face is smeared with dirt. I don't have any shoes on. I look like the drenched, mud-spattered family dog no one wants in their nice clean house. From the horrified look on his face, the usher certainly doesn't want me anywhere near his nice clean cathedral. He tries to bar my way. I don't have time to plead my case. I duck under his outstretched arm and scamper inside.

Up on the altar, a boy with a huge mop of frizzy hair, wearing an ill-fitting purple suit, holds a piece of paper in a trembling hand. In the other, he clutches a stuffed giraffe.

"And so good-bye, my old friend," reads the boy. "Our journey is at an end. But I will always think of your strong back and sturdy legs."

The boy drops the giraffe on the ground and stomps on him until the stuffing bursts and an eye pops out. The assembled guests cheer and applaud. Some of them weep. This, I'm guessing, is Atom Tubaldina's coming-of-age ritual. The poor kid has to destroy his favorite toys to show that he's a man. Two men carry a Lego city onto the altar. They carefully lower it to the ground. Atom looks down at it. I follow his gaze. From what I can see, it's an intricately constructed cityscape, complete with lines of cars sitting in traffic, bridges, towers, shops, and a public park. A lot of love, care, planning, and most of all time was clearly put into the building of this colorful city. And because of the requirements of his coming-of-age ceremony, Atom is about to stomp all over his young life's work. He looks at his sheet of paper and then down at his Lego city. He totally doesn't want to destroy it.

There's a loud cough from the congregation. Atom looks up. A man, presumably his father, the secretary of state, gives him an impatient *hurry up* hand gesture. Atom has this look on his face that I completely recognize. *I am on the verge of being a grown-up*, it says. *I know that I am expected to act like an adult and to make everyone watching me proud. But I feel like crying.*

"These are not real streets," he starts to read. "These are not real people. They do not live in real houses. . . ." Atom takes big gulps of air between lines. His face is starting to redden. I feel bad for him. Not just because I know, somewhere in this church, Vanessa Dominion is gearing up to shoot him, but because he is about to destroy something he holds dear. And for what? So he can mark what someone decided was the passage from childhood to adulthood? So a tradition can survive? Not all traditions deserve to survive.

"Good-bye, Lego city," whispers Atom. "It is time to leave you behind and live in the real world."

He looks down at the streets he built. He lifts up his foot. I can feel him willing himself not to break down and sob.

I pull back an arm and throw Red at the nearest stained-glass window.

As it shatters, I yell, "Gun!"

Atom freezes mid-stomp. Heads turn my way. I point dramatically at the broken window. The usher rushes toward me.

"She did it," he starts to say, but Red bounces back from the window and hits him in the forehead before he can get out another word. The usher keels over and drops to the ground.

Murmurs of fear turn to screams of terror as I hear the word *gun* repeated over and over. The occupants of both sides of the cathedral are on their feet. Trezekhastanis and Savlostavians yell and shake fists at one another. The cops start grabbing guests and pushing them toward the door.

"We need to clear the cathedral right now," they shout.

Scared guests stampede toward the door. I pretend I'm running along with them but I make a quick turn to the left before I'm swallowed up by the crowd and head up an empty row.

At the altar, Atom stares, confused and horrified at the frantic exodus from his Festival of Impending Manhood. His parents hurry to the altar to protect him. His mother grabs him and enfolds him in her arms. Atom's father, the secretary of state, looks down at the Lego city, shakes his head, and starts to lift his foot.

Bad dad!

I hurl Red. He hits Atom's father on the kneecap. He howls in pain and collapses on the ground. Atom and his mother scream in horror. It occurs to me that I might be a little too zealous in protecting Atom's Lego city.

I reach the end of the row and start running toward the altar. I keep my head down and stay in the shadows under the stained-glass windows.

One of the cops suddenly tumbles backward and falls down the stone steps. The second cop pulls his gun and puts himself in front of Atom and his mother. This guy I feel bad for because I know his impending fate. Ouch! His head jerks to one side, as if an invisible foot has struck it with great force. Ouch again! The cop doubles up and then falls to the ground. Atom stands defiantly in front of his mother and wounded—by me!—father.

"You want me," he shouts, "come and get me!"

Without having to destroy his Lego city, Atom has come of age!

Unfortunately for me, what Atom Tubaldina sees when he makes this defiant statement is me, charging toward the steps, reaching a hand inside my soaked jacket and pulling out what he probably thinks is a gun.

"It's not a gun!" I yell as I hurl the plastic soap dispenser from the cathedral's ladies' room straight at him.

Atom does not know this. He drops to the ground and throws his hands over his face. He hears the gunshot but he does not see the soap dispenser explode in midair. He does not see the liquid soap inside the dispenser spurt out and start to take shape as it dribbles and slides downward. He does not see the girl inside the soapy shape.

"It's in my mouth," splutters a disgusted English accent.

And then I see her. Vanessa: hair, face, black dress, and fancy shoes with perilously high heels all covered in liquid soap. She makes a nauseated throat-clearing sound and spits soap from her mouth. Her gun dangles from one hand as she rubs her eyes and slicks back her hair with the other one.

"Go!" I yell at Atom as I charge up the steps. Atom's mother helps lift his father from the ground. Atom rushes to assist her.

"Never mind him," I shout. "Get the Lego city to safety!"

Atom gives me a *who are you?* stare.

"I love Lego!" I shout back. I'm trying to express solidarity and empathy, but from the freaked-out look on his face, it absolutely fails to register with him.

Atom looks away from me and gathers up the Lego city as best he can while his parents hobble their way to the exit at the back of the church. Vanessa whirls on him and aims her gun. I run forward, snatch up the priest's thick prayer book, and use it to hit Vanessa under her elbow. The gun goes off, sending a bullet through the cathedral roof. Vanessa moves toward Atom, but I throw myself forward and wrap my arms around her ankles, bringing her crashing down to the ground.

"Ow ow ow ow!" she yelps.

I've got her! I won!

Her ankles shoot forward and slip straight out of my arms. She has both palms pressed onto the ground and seems to be doing some kind of reverse squat thrust. Maybe I haven't won? Her feet come flying back at me—nope, definitely haven't won—catching me in the stomach, lifting me off my feet, and sending me rolling down the steps. I land on top of the two cops.

"This has been fun, peanut," Vanessa says as she walks toward me, gun pointed at my head. "You're a feisty little critter. I'll miss you. I mean, I'll hit you. But after that, I'll miss you."

I drag myself off the cop who broke my fall. I hear him wince with pain as my hand pushes into his ribs.

"Sorry," I whisper.

Vanessa reaches the bottom step. "How about I give you a head start?" She smiles. "A sporting chance. Count of three. You run and hide. After that, bang bang."

"That's what you want your daddy to hear about?" I say. "That you were all talk? That you failed? You're no Irina O. You're Vanessa Ewww." (Even with a gun inches from my face, I'm still funny.)

"I know what you're doing," Vanessa says, but her smile looks strained. "You're trying to buy yourself a little time. Won't work."

She's right. I am. I keep going. "You couldn't kill Atom and his Lego city. So what's your consolation prize? A painfully average middle school student? That's the only job Edward Dominion thought you were capable of completing. And he was right. You showed him nothing. You showed me nothing."

Now she's angry. "Shut up, peanut," she snarls.

I don't. "We had tea, you know, Edward and I, tea and cakes. He liked me; he confided in me. He addressed me by my name. You know, the name my parents gave me. I've got a lot of people who care about me, Vanessa. What've you got?"

Splashes of red appear on Vanessa's cheeks.

"A gun," she says. But we both see her hand tremble. She changes to a two-handed grip.

"I promised you a count of three," she says. "Three. Two. One."

She pulls the trigger. I hurl myself to the floor. As I do, I see the gun fly over my head and embed itself in the ground halfway down the aisle. I also see the piece of pink half-chewed magnetic gum lying a few inches away from it. I gasp in shock. Irina.

Vanessa lets out a shriek of frustration and runs up the aisle. I spring to my feet and scramble after her. She spins around and kicks me. Her leg connects with my head and I see actual cartoon stars. I stumble into the nearest row, fall over a seat, and hit the ground.

"Irina," I mutter. "If you're here, now would be a good time to show yourself."

I look up to see a uniformed cop come charging through the cathedral door. He dives forward, grabs the gun off the ground, jumps to his feet, and aims the gun straight at Vanessa, who stumbles to a halt.

"Don't move," says Ryan.

# CHAPTER THIRTY-FOUR

# *Chameleon*

That is correct. My brother is dressed like an officer of the New York Police Department and he is
pointing a gun at Vanessa.

"Ryan?" I say from my place on the ground. I try to
get up but my head is still spinning from that last kick.

"Turns out Sam had an actual cop uniform in his
closet." He shrugs. "You okay? You're all wet. And you
smell. Not your usual smell. Worse."

"Red blew up the toilet," I tell him. "He did that
thing you used to do with the golf ball."

"Classic prank," says Ryan. "I've got to get one of
those marbles."

"Ryan," says Vanessa.

Uh-oh.

"So the bad guy knows my name," smirks Ryan.

"And you know me," she says.

"Ryan, you did great, but you need to go now," I tell him.

"Ryan," Vanessa whispers.

"Wait," says Ryan. "Are you . . . ?"

And she transforms. I don't know how she does it, but right in front of us, Vanessa changes. Her posture, her voice. Her mouth gets smaller, her toes point inward, she seems to shrink. She may even have changed the color of her eyes.

"Abby?" breathes Ryan.

"It's not Abby," I say. "There is no Abby. There never was. Her name is Vanessa Dominion. She's the under-achieving daughter of a criminal mastermind. She stuck a needle in you and hung you on a hook."

"That true?" he says. "You did that to me?"

Using her tiny, mumbly Abby voice, Vanessa says, "I did it to keep you safe. I would never hurt you, Ryan, you know that."

"You don't know that," I tell him. "Everything she ever said to you was a lie."

"Not everything," says Vanessa. "I never lied about how I felt."

I see Ryan's face cloud with confusion.

"Ryan, give me the gun and get out of here," I tell him. "You can't be around her."

"Bridget never liked me," says Vanessa, walking slowly toward him. "She doesn't know what we have, the two of us."

"You have nothing," I say to Ryan. "Abby doesn't exist. This is someone you don't know. Someone who just tried to kill me."

"Give me the gun," Vanessa tells Ryan. "I'll get us out of here. We can disappear and start a new life together."

I pull myself to my feet. "Ryan, don't fall for this."

Vanessa moves closer to him, close enough that she could reach out and take the gun from him, which is what I very much fear she's going to do. Vanessa's firmly in Blabby mode now, speaking so quietly I can't make out a word.

"But how can I ever trust you again?" says Ryan, and then he says, "You swear? You'll never hurt anyone again?"

"NO!" I bawl. "Don't be so stupid; she's exploiting your weakness. You're nothing to her. You were never anything but a means to get to me."

Ryan turns to me, a furious look on his face. "Right. Because no one could ever like me. Because everything's got to be about you, Bridget."

Vanessa takes the gun from Ryan in one blurry movement. One second it was in his hand, the next it's in hers, and she's pointing it at him.

"NO!" I bawl again, and put myself between Vanessa and Ryan.

"And here we are again," says Vanessa.

"Abby," says Ryan, aghast.

I feel bad for him, but at the same time I'm incensed. "Stop calling her Abby! Don't you get it? Haven't you been listening to a word I've said?"

Vanessa laughs her musical little laugh. "I'm flattered," she says to Ryan. "Abby made an indelible impression on you, as she was intended to do. Because your sister is absolutely right: you were a means to an end."

I see Ryan struggle to understand. His shoulders slump and he hangs his head.

"Awww," she mocks. "Don't be sad. Abby really liked you."

Every time I think I've reached the depths of my hatred for Vanessa, she pushes me deeper.

"Like you said, peanut, you've got a lot of people who care about you, which means you'll always be weak," she smirks.

I glance upward so I don't have to see her eyes

mocking my rage. That's when I spot clouds of what looks like sawdust drifting down from above. The dust is being expelled from a wooden beam that stretches across the ceiling. The beam is starting to splinter and break. Ryan and Vanessa follow my gaze. They see what I see. The wooden beam breaks in two. The air ripples. The outline of a human body begins to form as it falls to the ground. Vanessa aims her gun. Irina lands in front of me and snatches the weapon from Vanessa's hand. I see the frayed rope knotted around her wrists and ankles.

"That's right," says Irina, keeping her eyes on Vanessa. "She soaked me in the cloaking liquid and hung me upside down from the cathedral ceiling so I could watch her shoot my target. It was cold and calculating. Exactly the sort of thing I would have done."

"Well, of course, I'm such a fan of your work," gushes Vanessa with the biggest, brightest smile on her face.

"Take your brother and get out of here," Irina says, her face grim. "Miss Dominion and I have unfinished business."

"I'd love to pick your brains about the whole assassin thing," chirps Vanessa. "I have so much to learn."

"And so little time," says Irina.

I see fear flash across Vanessa's face. I was too slow. Ryan was too confused. Irina won't be either of these things. Wiping out Vanessa will be like sneezing to her. I take Ryan's arm.

"Come on," I say.

"Hey, Ryan," Irina suddenly calls out. He looks around at her.

"You can do better."

I watch the defeat start to leave Ryan's face. He stands a little straighter. I wish I'd been the one to do that for him.

"Who is that?" he says as we head for the doors.

"She gave birth to me," I say.

"Despite that, I like her," he says. "Where's she been hiding all these years?"

"I'll tell you the whole story," I say, pushing him up the aisle and toward the door. "But right now, you and I need to leave here and we need to not look back."

So we look straight ahead. We see the cathedral doors burst open and a hundred cops swarm in, all with weapons drawn. Ryan and I both raise our hands in surrender.

"Put the gun down now," screams a cop through his bullhorn.

Behind us, we hear a gun go off.

# CHAPTER THIRTY-FIVE

# The Fast and the Furious

"That little brat stole my arrow-shooting gun thing!" screams Irina.

I whirl around in time to see Vanessa—or at least her shoes—disappear through the hole in the cathedral roof.

Irina, who does not look anywhere in the neighborhood of pleased, aims another of her many hidden weapons at the hole.

"The gun, now!" bawls the cop through his bullhorn.

Irina lowers her gun to the ground, kicks it in the direction of the cops, and raises both hands.

The army of NYPD officers charges up the aisle.

One of them slows down and jabs a finger at Ryan.

"Get that child out of here," he barks.

Ryan doesn't move.

"He means you have to get me out of here," I whisper to my brother.

Ryan grins widely. That officer just made the biggest mistake of his life. He validated Ryan's belief that he can pass as a New York City cop.

"Come with me, anonymous dripping child," Ryan booms as he starts pushing me toward the cathedral doors. I shake him off and look back at Irina. Before she's completely swamped by cops, she meets my gaze and gives me a pained shrug.

My blood boils. It actually boils. On the one hand, I'm impressed by Vanessa's resilience. On the other hand, this will not stand. Vanessa Dominion has played havoc with the lives of my family. She does not get to enjoy another day unpunished for her crimes. She does not get to regroup. Her reign of terror ends here and it ends at my hands.

I pull away from Ryan and tear out of the cathedral, past the crowds of traumatized guests who are milling around on the other side of the police barricades. I'm vaguely aware of Ryan trying to find me among the mass of bodies, but I'm also in the grip of a righteous fury that shows no sign of abating.

I cross the street and crane my neck up to the roof of the cathedral. I have a trained eye. I see what the average non-spy does not. If Vanessa is lurking in the shadows waiting for the crowds to disperse, I will see her. If she tries to climb down the front or side walls, I will see her. I can wait for her to show herself. I will not be distracted.

A sudden swelling of boos and jeers distracts me from my roof-staring duties. Irina, hands cuffed behind her back, is being marched toward a waiting police van. The assembled Trezekhastanis and Savlostavians immediately forget that they're mortal enemies and direct their united hatred at my birth mother, who did nothing wrong.

"Leave her alone," I say out loud, but not loud enough for any angry guest to overhear.

From somewhere behind me, I hear a yell of pain. The yell is followed by the sound of a body hitting the ground. I rush around the corner of Twenty-Third and Eighth.

I see a guy lying dazed on the ground with a hand over his eye while a girl kicks his motorcycle into life with her perilously high-heeled shoes and roars away from me. I watch Vanessa zoom out of my life and I feel defeat.

Maybe I should be happy she got away. Maybe I

should just count the minutes till I'm back in Reindeer Crescent.

A car pulls up at the side of the street, inches from where I stand. A very small Smart Car driven by an old Chinese woman.

The passenger door opens. Dale Tookey is at the wheel. He's in my car! The self-driving, self-camouflaging design given to me by Section 23.

"You knew I couldn't sit back and leave it to the cops," I say as I clamber inside.

"I made an educated guess," he says.

"Nothing's changed here," says the high, screechy voice of the car that sounds nothing like me. "You mess up, we show up in the nick of time to save you."

"Hi, car," I mutter.

"Wait," says the car. "Something's changed." It makes a sniffing noise. "You smell like an old man's underwear."

"A toilet exploded under me," I explain.

"Not for the first time," says the car.

I roll down my window.

"I did the right thing, though," I say to Dale. "If it wasn't for me, Atom Tubaldina would be dead and his Lego city destroyed."

"Do you mean his legacy?" Dale asks.

"The cops couldn't have stopped Vanessa," I continue. "Only I could."

"When you've finished patting yourself on your smelly back with your smelly hand," says the car, "you might want to stop talking and try catching her."

"She's not getting away," says Dale.

He starts the car and focuses on the digital street plan of Manhattan on the computer screen built into the dashboard.

"Vanessa's the worst," I tell Dale. "She's a selfish, arrogant, violent psycho desperate to live up to her father's legacy."

"Smells like someone we know," says the car.

"Who? Me?" I immediately squeal. "I'm nothing like her. She's the epitome of evil. I'm awesome. I help everyone. I save lives. Dale, am I anything like her? 'You're not' should be the first words out of your mouth."

"You're not," Dale says.

I relax back into the seat and enjoy the pursuit.

"You're not because you're half a spy," he says.

"What's that now?" I say, unsure whether I heard him right.

"This Vanessa is all the way in," Dale says. "You're not. You think you can be a spy when it suits you and then go back to your normal life. But you can't. If you're a part-time spy, you're always going to be playing catch-up. You'll always be the last to know the latest intel. You'll always be the last to get your hands on the latest gadgets. You have to commit or walk away, Bridget. You can't just show up for a weekend and then go back to school like nothing happened."

Am I getting a lecture here? Because it sounds like Dale Tookey is giving me a lecture.

"Wait," I say, trying to stay calm. "Last time we talked about this, all those many, many months ago, it was you, Dale Tookey, who told me, Bridget Wilder, not to get sucked into the spy life. If you remember that far back."

"I remember," says Dale, staring straight ahead. "I thought you made the right decision, but now you're in New York playing spy with your new friends."

"My new . . . ," I begin. I don't finish the sentence. Dale's acting weird at the weirdest possible time. He's acting weird in the middle of a pursuit. We've been in a car chase in this very vehicle before and he didn't act weird. Why the weirdness now?

"Because he saw the way another boy looked at you," says the car.

"Shut up, car!" growls Dale.

"No," I gasp. "Really? That's it?"

"That's not it," says Dale, his face reddening. "Forget it."

"He never texted, he never called," I tell the car. "Months went by. Nothing."

"Months went by without a Sam taking you out on a date," says the car.

"It's not a *date* date," I tell Dale.

He stares at the digital street map.

"You know Sam's MO," I say. "He did me a favor, I had to promise him something in return. But whatever we end up doing, I'll bring Joanna. It won't be fun for anyone."

Dale keeps looking at the red dot as it takes the corner at the next street. We follow in uncomfortable silence. The car turns on its radio stations, flipping channels until it settles on an old song called "The Girl Is Mine" where the singers pretend they're fighting over some chick.

I turn down the volume. The car turns it back up.

"I'm not playing this game with you, car," I say.

The car switches stations until it settles on another old song. This one's called "Jealous Guy."

Again I go to mute the song. Again the stupid car turns it back up. I sit in sullen silence and think about how excited I was to see Dale in the Chinese restaurant. How did that feeling turn into this?

"We got her," Dale says suddenly.

He points to his screen. "Roadwork up ahead. The traffic's down to one lane. There's nowhere for her to go."

And just like that, we're not fighting anymore. I'm confused by how fast feelings can change, but I like that Dale's stopped being weird. I like that Vanessa's escape plan looks like it's being foiled by something as mundane as a hole in the road.

And now we can see her and—yes!—she's stuck behind a garbage truck.

"Appropriate," Dale and I say at the same time. We both laugh. We're totally in the groove here. The previous weirdness is just a memory.

Vanessa pulls her stolen motorcycle onto the sidewalk. She starts plowing through a sea of people. As I watch her, I think back to the way I tore up the sidewalk on a stolen skateboard earlier this afternoon but, again, we are nothing alike.

The garbage truck ahead of us starts moving. I unbuckle my seat belt.

"Get me close to her," I tell Dale. "I'll jump out, kick her off the bike, and put her down for good."

Dale gives me a dubious look.

"You may think I'm half a spy," I say, my emotions

building. "But I'm the right half. I'm the half that saves lives. I'm the half that gets it done."

"I like that half," says Dale.

"Ugh," says the car.

Dale gets me close to the sidewalk. We draw up behind Vanessa. I open my door, and . . .

She drives the motorcycle straight through the open doors of a supermarket.

"Come on!" yells Dale.

"No no no no no!" I bawl. "She does not get to give us the slip. This is a small car. Small enough to follow her."

"No way," says Dale.

"No way!" yelps the car.

"This is happening," I screech. "We're doing it. We're going shopping!"

Dale, infected by my crazed enthusiasm, yanks the car onto the sidewalk and drives straight for the open doors of Fresh & Frozen Quality Foods.

"That British brat is past her sell-by date!" I shout, triumphantly.

# CHAPTER THIRTY-SIX

# Cleanup on Aisle Seven

It seemed like a good idea at the time. It even seemed like a good idea as the hood of the car rolled past the supermarket doors. But then we got wedged halfway through. The car made this screeching sound, and then we couldn't go any farther forward and we couldn't reverse out. Dale put his foot down. He gunned the engine. He couldn't get the car unstuck. And what's worse, we can't get out of the car. Our doors are jammed against the walls of Fresh & Frozen Quality Goods. We're trapped.

"Do something," yells the car, its voice suddenly crackling and distorted.

"I'm trying," says Dale. But there's not much he can do except rev the engine, and the more he does that, the more aware I become that our gas is not going to last forever. Or anywhere close to forever.

But we're not just sitting trapped in our small car. We have an amazing show playing out in front of us. From the comfort of our seats, we get to watch Vanessa ride her motorcycle into cheese displays and send towering displays of fruit flying. We get to watch Fresh & Frozen customers screaming in fear as she chases them around the aisles. We get to watch her throw a frozen chicken at the store security guard. A frozen chicken hurled from a moving motorcycle can be a deadly weapon.

And why is Vanessa destroying a supermarket? Because she knows I can't do anything but watch. Because she's turned me into her captive audience—again.

After she's done terrorizing the staff and customers, Vanessa pulls the bike over and leaves it with the shell-shocked manager of the deli counter. She takes off her helmet and picks up a banana from the ground.

Vanessa walks toward the car, her eyes on mine. She peels the top of the banana and takes a bite.

I pull out Red and throw him at her. He bounces straight off the windshield and flies back at my face. I scream in shock as he whistles past my ear.

"Shatterproof," says Dale.

Red bounces off the back window and comes flying at me again. I make a grab at him and shove him back in my pocket.

Vanessa struts right up to the car.

"Three steps ahead, peanut," she says.

Then she gives Dale a little pouty smile. "You can do better," she tells him.

Vanessa climbs up on the hood of the car. She stretches out a leg and lifts herself onto the roof. I hear her slide across. I squirm around in my tiny seat and watch her make her way down the trunk and back onto the ground. She holds up the banana for me to see, wiggles it in a good-bye gesture, and then she sticks it in the tail pipe. We were never going anywhere, but she couldn't resist one last slap in my face.

I watch Vanessa walk away, slowly and leisurely, because once again, she knows my eyes are on her.

"Sorry," says Dale.

"It's not your fault," I say, turning back around. And now I see he wasn't saying sorry to me. The staff and customers of Fresh & Frozen Quality Goods are heading toward the car. They do not look happy. Vanessa was a moving target. She had the element of surprise. We do not. We're stuck here.

I kick at my door. Useless, of course, but I can't just sit here. I've got all this anger building up in me. How could she do this to me again? I punch the dashboard. I punch the roof.

"Stop hit-hit-hit-hitting me," hiccups the car.

"How can this car speak, how can it drive itself, how can it have a fake driver in the window but it doesn't have a sunroof?" I yell.

A can of peaches hits the windshield. I scream in fright. The Fresh & Frozen mob has turned ugly. A can of peas follows. Then an egg splatters across the windshield. More eggs follow until a sheet of yolk and egg white acts as a curtain between us and the angry staff and customers.

"Stooooooop thrrrroooooooowwwwwing foooooood," groans the car, its voice slowing down and coming to a long moaning halt.

"I don't know if this is going to work," says Dale. "It probably won't."

"What?" I say.

"I found this," he says. "Lying on the highway. After the whole thing with Spool."

He holds a tube of lip balm out to me. Burned. Dented. But still recognizably . . .

"Smoky pear," I breathe.

I twist the bottom. Was it once for smoke, twice for Taser? I could never remember.

A laser beam shoots out. It burns a hole in the dashboard.

"Sorry," I say, wincing because I've caused the wounded car even more pain.

I point the laser up at the roof and turn it in a circle. Dale gets up and pushes both arms over his head. I join him. We make a hole. A hole big enough to climb out of.

"Bye, car," I say sadly as I take my leave. We had our differences, but I'll miss her.

I emerge from the roof of the trapped car to see a frozen chicken headed straight for my face. I whip my laser at the bird and it defrosts, smokes, and catches fire in seconds.

The angry mob freezes.

"I'm sorry about the mess," I say. "We won't pay for it and we won't help clean it up, but we're going to do something better. We're going to catch the perpetrator, we're going to drag her back here, and we're all going to throw eggs in her smug face! Who's with me?"

A few cheers. Not the hysteria I was hoping for. Whatever. I slide across the roof and down the trunk on to the ground. And now I start running.

I don't have to run far. Vanessa is only half a block

ahead of me and she's impossible to miss. Traffic is backed up and she's on the roofs of the cars, skipping from one to the next.

Incensed drivers honk their horns and shake their fists at her. Some climb out of their cars and try to catch her, but she's too fast. She keeps skipping from roof to roof.

And then Vanessa stops on the roof of a black Mercedes.

A rope ladder seems to drop from the sky and unfurls in front of her. She grabs it and starts to climb. The driver of the Mercedes gets out of his car and stares upward in disbelief. The other drivers trapped in the snarl-up do the same. Dale breathlessly catches up to me and says "Come on!" again.

He's right. What else is there to say when you watch your adversary making her latest escape up a ladder into a waiting helicopter?

I pull back a hand to throw Red at her but I know it's a fruitless gesture. I can't ask any more of the little guy, so I let my hand drop back down to my side. Dale takes it.

"There'll be another time," he says.

I nod. I know he's right. I need to accept this is over and move on.

But then I hear something. It's faint but it's high and piercing.

Laughter.

Vanessa's laughing at me.

Even from this distance, even over the roar of traffic and helicopter blades, I can hear her mocking, condescending, triumphant laughter. (Or maybe I'm just imagining it because—I don't know if I've mentioned this—I hate her so much.)

"This will not stand," I say out loud. "You do not get to make a cool getaway!"

# CHAPTER THIRTY-SEVEN

# Spy in the Sky

"Bridget, no!" yells Dale.

I know he knows what I'm about to do and I know he thinks it ranks at the top of my list of all-time terrible ideas. But I can't stop myself. I run into the street and clamber up on the trunk of a gray Honda idling in the long line of non-moving cars, and I run across the roof, spring onto the hood, and jump onto to the next car.

The same honks and shouts of anger that greeted Vanessa moments earlier are now aimed my way. I hear but I don't care. Rage fuels me: it makes me run faster and jump higher. I'm two cars away from the black Mercedes. Vanessa still hangs from the bottom rung of the rope ladder as the black helicopter hovers above the buildings. The roar of the chopper blades drowns out the car horns and the abuse hurled my way.

Vanessa holds on to the ladder by one hand, and with the other she brandishes her phone and takes what I'm sure are unflattering pictures of me with my arms flailing and my mouth hanging open. She looks up at the helicopter and mouths, "Let's go!"

But as I jump from a station wagon to the trunk of the black Mercedes, she's still hanging there.

"I said let's go!" she screams over the sound of the blades. The black helicopter starts to pull away. Vanessa begins climbing the ladder. I reach the roof of the black Mercedes but I know I'm too late. Frustration sweeps over me as I watch my nemesis fly out of my life.

"Get off my car," I hear the driver beneath me yell.

"It's her!" squeaks another voice.

A chorus of boos and jeers erupt from the minivan directly in front of me. A familiar head pops out of a window. A familiar head wearing a big bow and a look of disgust. More heads pop out. It's my old friends, the Bronze Canyon Valkyries!

"What are you doing here?" demands Big Bow. "Are

you trying to sabotage Classic Cheer? Is that next on your diabolical agenda?"

I start to laugh. Not a *ha-ha, isn't life hilarious in its randomness and unpredictability* laugh. More of a *just when I thought things couldn't get any worse, they just got worse* laugh.

I look up at my nemesis, Vanessa—my Vanemesis!—and then back at the angry, accusing faces of the Bronze Canyon Valkyries. And then I stop laughing.

"Hey, ladies," I shout. "Can I ask you to do me a favor?"

They gasp in unison.

"What? You want to steal another kitten?" asks the willowy blonde with the baby voice.

I point upward at Vanessa, who is still climbing the rope ladder.

"That girl making the cool getaway? She's the real culprit behind the Classic Cheer choreography blackmail scam thing. She set me up and she tried to steal your winning cheer. Help me bring her to justice."

"How?" demands Big Bow.

I leap from the Mercedes to the roof of the minivan.

"Get me up there," I say.

The faces of the Bronze Canyon Valkyries look confused.

"Why would we do that?" demands the willowy blonde.

"Look at it this way," I shout down at them. "If you don't throw me high enough, I fall to my death. If you throw me too high, I get decapitated by the helicopter blades. It's a win-win for you."

Instantly, Big Bow squeezes out of the window and joins me on the roof of the minivan. From below, I hear the other cheerleaders fight for the honor of tossing me to my death. The willowy blonde is the victor. She joins Big Bow on the roof. They link hands. The rest of the Valkyries spill out onto the street and break into a hip-shaking, hand-clapping routine, which, I'm sure, the traffic-jammed motorists appreciate.

"Seriously," I tell them. "Try not to kill me."

I step onto their linked hands. *Is stopping Vanessa's escape worth this?* I ask myself, and then I remember how much I detest her, and let them lift me effortlessly into the air.

"One," says Big Bow.

"Two," says the willowy blonde.

"Three!" they both scream and hurl me upward.

These are strong girls. I feel the wind on my face as I rocket skyward.

From far beneath me, I hear a collective "Oooh!"

The Valkyries are either scared for my safety or antici-pating my imminent demise. I reach out a hand and grab the bottom rung of the rope ladder. I swing a leg up and almost touch the ladder. The rope swings out into the air as the helicopter pulls away. I close my eyes and try to remain calm and focused. Then I try again. This time I kick as far as I can go. My leg hits the bottom rung of the ladder. I pull myself into a standing position and then I feel a stabbing pain in my fingers. A perilously high heel is jabbing into my hand.

"Sorry, peanut, no room for you," Vanessa shouts down at me. Her heel comes down toward my hand. I let go of the ladder for a split second and then grab the back of her shoe.

Vanessa screams in fright and tries to shake me off. The black helicopter is now pulling up high over the city and I am hanging on for dear life with one foot on the ladder and one hand on the back of Vanessa's shoe. The roar of the chopper blades deafens me. The wind in my face is blinding. On the plus side, I don't have to worry about looking down. All I can do is cling on as tightly as I'm able.

"Get off me," I hear Vanessa shriek in a voice so huge and filled with fear and anger it overpowers the thunder-ous noise of the helicopter. The more she tries to kick me away, the harder I grip. I grip so hard that I pull her shoe off and I'm left grabbing air. For a second, I think, *That's it. That's me. I'm over*, but sheer determination pushes me forward. I claw at the wind and I am rewarded with a handful of rope. I pull myself up with both hands and manage to get my feet on the bottom rung. Above me, I see Vanessa with her one shoe and one bare foot, climbing to the top of the ladder and pulling herself into the helicopter.

She looks down at me and shakes her head in what I would like to think of as admiration at my tenacity. There's a vast bubbling cauldron of hate between us but, weirdly, also a small amount of mutual respect. Vanessa thought I was a joke. Now she sees me as a worthy adversary. From her, I've learned to step up my game, to never be complacent, and to be prepared to face the worst the enemy has to offer. Like now, for instance.

Vanessa smiles down from the inside of the helicopter. She brandishes a small knife and shows me what she plans to do with it. She mimes cutting the rope ladder, and then she sets about actually doing it. Can I get up the ladder before she hacks the top ropes to shreds? I don't know. I feel a bit like my friend the car as she ran out of gas. My limbs are heavy. I don't have the energy to haul myself up the steps that stretch out above me. Hanging on to the ladder as it sways from side to side is making me nauseous.

"That's right, peanut, you give up," I hear Vanessa's voice giggle above me. "Have a rest. You deserve it. You put up a nice little fight. I commend you. But now I've got to let you go."

I put up a good fight, but it wasn't enough. I don't know that I've got anything left to give.

It might be my imagination, but from far beneath me, I think I hear voices, angelic voices.

"Let's go, Bridget!"

*Clap-clap.*

Is that . . . can it be the Bronze Canyon Valkyries cheering me on?

"Let's go, Bridget!"

*Clap-clap. Clap-clap-clap.*

Now, maybe by *let's go,* they mean *hurry up and fall to your death,* but I choose to believe they're encouraging me. Their belief relights my dimming fire. Maybe I do have a little fight left in me.

Vanessa continues sawing away at the rope ladder. I reach into my pocket for my dented, burned lip balm. I twist the bottom three times. A plume of smoke wafts out like a breath on a cold day. That's it? I twist again. A limp laser beam shoots out a few inches and then wilts and vanishes. I can't fault the gadget. It gave me what little life it had left.

I twist one more time and the Taser setting I never used explodes out of the tube, firing an electrode straight toward Vanessa. She shrieks and tumbles backward inside the helicopter. I haul my tired arms up the ladder and climb as fast as I can. I reach the top and jump inside the open door.

Vanessa lies in a gasping, panicky heap on the ground between the two rows of passenger seats.

"Bridget Wilder," says the pilot in a cultured, amused voice I find instantly familiar.

"Sir Edward," I say, taking in his white hair and dark glasses. "I mean, Edward." Why do I keep calling him Sir Edward?

"Kill her," yells Vanessa. "Throw her out of the helicopter. Squash her like the insect she is!"

"Why would we do that," Edward says, "when we could use her to our advantage?"

"How?" says Vanessa, pulling herself up to sit on a chair.

"Yeah, how?" I say. I feel suddenly trapped and vulnerable. Two Dominions and one me in a helicopter. There's no easy way out this time.

"Imagine the satisfaction of bringing her to our side,

finding out how she thinks, extracting information about who she works for, taking all she's been taught, and using it to further our cause. Wouldn't that be interesting?"

Vanessa glows at being treated as an equal, at being noticed.

She gives me a slow, taunting smile. "Very interesting."

"I'm not talking to you," he says.

Vanessa looks confused. "Who are you talking to?"

Edward removes his dark glasses. His eyes vanish, leaving a strip of static. The rest of his features freeze and fade away. He raises a hand to his neck, pushes a finger to his chin, and his face falls off.

"My daughter," says Carter Strike.

"Nanomask!" I shout.

"Nanomask," he agrees, and pulls off the white wig.

I see Vanessa's mouth drop open.

"Four steps ahead, Blabby," I crow. I'm lying. Strike's appearance is as big a shock to me as it is to her, but I figure I'm allowed to enjoy the moment.

"The CIA has your father," Strike tells Vanessa. "The Forties is out of business. Now we have to figure out what to do with you."

Vanessa looks from me to Strike. I see the emotions fly across her face. First, she's stunned. Then a little bit weepy. Now she starts calculating. What angle can she work here? What character can she become? What weakness can she exploit? I see her features soften. Her eyes moisten. She clasps her hands together.

"I feel like I never really had a father," she says to Strike in a wispy little voice. "Someone I could look up to. Someone who could show me right from wrong. You're a kind man, Mr. Strike, I can tell that just by looking at you. I'd like to learn from you. I'd like to . . . ow ow ow ow!"

Yeah, I threw Red at her. He bounced off her forehead—not enough to knock her out, just enough to shut her up. Just enough to let her know I won. We won. I get up to join Strike. As I rise, I hear a knock on the door. A knock on the outside of the helicopter door.

"Get that, would you?" he says, giving me a grin.

I slide the door open and Irina climbs in.

"Oh God," moans Vanessa.

"You got away from me once," says Irina. "That's not going to happen again."

"Miss Ouspenskaya," Vanessa pleads. "I never had a mother. Someone to teach me right from wrong."

Irina cracks her knuckles. "Lesson one. What I'm about to do is wrong."

Vanessa gives me an imploring stare. "Don't let her hurt me."

"A minute ago you wanted me thrown off the heli-copter," I remind her.

"That's our thing." Vanessa laughs desperately. "Our funny back-and-forth."

"Sit down, Irina O," says Strike. "No one's killing anyone." He gestures to his earpiece. "I just got word from the CIA. Vanessa's being placed in a facility."

"Wh-what kind of facility?" she stammers.

"A place where you'll be very happy," says Strike.

"Or very unhappy," says Irina.

"Most likely very unhappy," agrees Strike.

Any fight left in Vanessa vanishes. She hugs herself and rocks back and forth in her seat.

I almost feel sorry for her. Almost

Irina sits down next to me and takes my hands in hers.

"Okay, now, we're going to spend some time together. We've got till Monday, so what do you want to do?"

"Well," I say, "I've got this date I'm supposed to go on. I really need to find something to wear."

"Date?" says Strike. "Aren't you a little young for that?"

"You think you have any say?" says Irina. "We'll find you something special for your date. Something that'll knock his eyes out. Not literally."

Irina starts to plan our extensive shopping trip. As she talks, I catch Vanessa watching us out of the corner of her eye. She looks sullen and contemptuous. I have nothing more to say to her. But if I felt like talking, I'd say, *Having people who care about you doesn't make you weak, it makes you strong.*

# CHAPTER THIRTY-EIGHT

# *The Date*

"You look nice," says Sam. He's a little less confident than usual. A little less cool. A tiny bit nervous. "I mean, you always look nice. But tonight, you just . . . there's something about you. It's like you're lit from within. I know that sounds corny. You bring that out in me. I feel like I don't have to put on a front when I'm around you."

"What means front?" says Zamira Kamirov, Sam's beautiful date for the evening.

Oh, I'm sorry. Did you think he was talking to me? Nope. Sam and Zamira hit it off so well during their afternoon of fun and excitement in Manhattan that he pretended to release me from my debt of having to go on a date with him so he could cling on to Zamira's hand in case she floated back to heaven.

And that's fine by me. I was never going to go on a date with Sam. Well, not just him. If Sam had held me to it, I would have agreed to go out with him, but I would also have insisted on bringing Ryan, Joanna, Dale, Strike, and Irina, the people who meant the most to me during this frantic, terrifying trip to New York. As it turns out, I get to do just that.

Strike and Irina accompanied me to Brooklyn on Sunday afternoon so I could hang out with Joanna and present Alex Gunnery with a bunch of flowers as an apology for abusing her hospitality over the course of the weekend (and also for stealing and destroying her clothes, which I will not be telling her about). By this time, Joanna had convinced her to stop hating me. In fact, Alex had huge plans for my last night in New York.

"You're so lucky you came here when you did. There's an incredible festival of the best local musicians Brooklyn has to offer tonight at the bandshell."

Alex took a breath and waited for my excited reaction. When I failed to provide one, she started yammering again.

"The Brooklyn Bandshell? In Prospect Park? The celebrated outdoor venue? I know you've heard of it. Legends perform there. Giants."

"Actual giants?" asked Irina, giving me a nudge.

"Blues guitarists, reggae bands, singer-songwriters, zydeco legends, old-school rap heroes. I'll bet there'll be some clog dancers . . . ," Alex said, her eyes widening with every fresh genre she named.

"That sounds incredible," said Strike. "But we've got tickets for . . ."

I could see Strike's mind race. He said "the Knicks" at the exact same moment Irina said "the opera."

It was painfully obvious they were both lying.

I saw the wounded look in Alex's eyes and punched Strike in the arm. "He's such a kidder," I told her. "We'd love to go. Thank you so much." I'd told enough lies for a lifetime these past few days. Why not relish the opportunity to spend time doing something relatively normal with no threat to anyone's life?

So this is where we are. Sitting in front of a huge shell-shaped stage while some half-blind, almost-dead blues legend plays guitar with his teeth. And he's the liveliest act in the entire show so far. But I don't care. I'm sitting next to Dale. We're sharing a pizza and we've got tonight and a bit of tomorrow before I go home.

"Worst music ever," I say.

"Never heard anything as horrible," he agrees. I let my head rest on his shoulder.

After a moment, he says, "This security job I'm doing. It's not going to last forever."

"It'd be pretty weird if it did," I say. "You'd be an old toothless man still pretending to be a hacker."

"What I'm saying is, I probably won't stay in New York. I might come back to California."

"But you don't know," I say. "You don't know for sure. You might get another job you can't say no to."

"Yes, but . . . ," he starts to say.

"And I don't want you to say no," I tell him. "I just want to know you're okay. I just want to hear your voice and get your texts and know wherever you are and whatever you're doing, there's a moment when you're thinking of me."

"There's more than a moment," Dale says. "There's always more than a moment."

And with the sound of an ancient blues guitarist making his instrument bleat like a dying lamb, Dale and I kiss.

"Oooohhh," chorus the concertgoers seated around us.

"Careful," I hear Ryan yell. "She's still got bits of toilet on her."

"She's got little bits of Squirrel as well," laughs Sam.

Dale pulls away from me. "Too public," he says. "Too many people."

He gets up.

"You're going?" I say. "You're always going."

Dale gestures around the crowded park. "I'm under-cover," he says. "Everyone's got a camera, everyone's got a microphone. All those phones freak me out."

However upset I feel by his desire to leave, I can't say I don't understand. We spies live in a weird world. We can't trust anyone we don't know. At least I had this time with him. At least I know we both still feel the same.

"I'm Bluey Harvest and this is my brother, Creech," drawls a voice from the bandshell. The old blues guitarist I will forever associate with my most recent kiss has left the stage. Two skinny dudes who wear faded dungarees and carry acoustic guitars gather around a microphone. "We're gonna play a song by the Louvin Brothers," says one. "Hope y'all like it."

The skinny dudes strum a few chords, and then they start to sing in harmony. "If I could only win your love," they whine.

"Geese," I fume.

"What?" says Dale.

A few seats down from me, Strike stands and holds

his hand out to Irina. She gets up and they slow-dance to the song. Little Lucien jumps up and holds his hand out to Joanna, who is not even a bit embarrassed; she gets right up and dances with the kid. Sam and Zamira are next. They make a lovely couple. Alex watches them with tears in her eyes. I see her search the row for an available man. Her gaze falls on Ryan. He puts his phone to his ear. "What's that? Armed robbery in progress on Atlantic Avenue? I'll be right there." He makes a sorry face to Alex and runs off.

Which leaves me and Dale as the only non-dancers in our party.

"I know you've got to go," I say.

"Maybe one dance," he says.

So we hold each other for the duration of this terrible song I will never get out of my head. (Thanks, Louvin Brothers, whoever you may be.) I feel him close to me, his arms around my waist, my hands around his neck. When he's gone, I'll still have this feeling, and I'll hold on to it for a long, long time. When the song ends, I applaud with everyone else and I don't look around to see Dale slip away. But I do raise my hand and do a five-finger spider wiggle.

I feel someone touch my shoulder.

"That guy keeps running away from you," Joanna

says. "You must be a horrible kisser."

"The worst," I agree.

"If it's any consolation, no one's going to want to kiss you when you're back at Reindeer Crescent," she says.

"That's a relief."

"But I'll be around to walk you to school," she says.

I turn and stare at her.

"Big Log's on the mend," she says. "She'll be home soon."

"That's great." I smile. "That's the best news."

But it isn't. Joanna's eyes are watery. She chews her bottom lip. I see her glance in Alex's direction and then look over at little Lucien, who is gobbling a plate of ice cream. She does not want to leave this.

"You can come back and visit," I tell her. "You can come back all the time. It'll be something to look forward to."

"Not the same," Joanna mutters.

"Jojo, come danthe," squeals Lucien, running toward her.

"Coming, monster," she says, wiping her eyes and putting on a happy face.

I feel horrible for my friend. I see Sam and Zamira, both looking gorgeous, taking pictures of their gorgeousness. *That could have been you*, a little voice in my head says. *You and him looking gorgeous together. He wouldn't have run out on you. He would have made a clog dance contest movie for you.*

"No knot," I tell the little voice.

"No what?" says Strike, who wanders up to join me. Irina is by his side and they're both smiling at me. "Can we talk for a minute?" he says.

I nod.

"Somewhere a little more private," says Irina.

Oh my God. They're getting back together.

We walk around the back of the bandshell.

I wait for them to break the big news.

Strike looks at Irina. She looks back at him. He nods and takes a breath.

"This is hard," he says. "It's not something I thought would happen to me. Not at this stage in my life."

"When you're so old and slow," says Irina.

"You want to tell her?" says Strike. "Be my guest."

"Tell me what?" I demand. I'm already thinking, Will they move to Sacramento? Will they want me to spend some of the year in New York with them? What about school? What do I tell Mom and Dad?

"The Forties isn't out of business," says Strike.

"What's that now?" I say. This wasn't what I was expecting to hear.

"That's not how you start," snaps Irina. "What happened was . . ."

"The CIA sees the Forties as an amazing resource," says Strike. "The people under its umbrella, the innovations in tech and weaponry, the client list, and so . . ."

"And so they thought, why let all the warlords, billionaires, corrupt politicians, and crooked cops who use the services of the Forties look elsewhere?" says Irina.

"Why not keep it open?" says Strike. "Or at least, pretend to keep it open."

"Like a fake Forties?" I say. "A faux-rties?"

"You're so smart," Irina says, smiling.

"Yeah, a counterfeit Forties," says Strike. "With a bootleg boss running the fake show."

"You?" I say. "But you're done with spying; you're an old, burned-out spy. Your words."

"The CIA doesn't think so," says Irina. "They think there's life in the old dog. They think there's life in me, too."

"You'd be running this knock-off Forties together?" I say.

They both nod.

I don't even know what to say about this. I don't think I like it. But I remember the mess Strike made of his life when he wasn't a spy. Maybe it's the only thing he's good at. But Irina?

"You were out," I say. "You were going to sing."

"It's a younger woman's game," she says. "This is a chance to make up for the bad things I did. This is a chance to work for the right side."

"The CIA tried to kill you, both of you," I remind them.

"And now they trust us so much they put us in charge," says Strike.

"Well, good luck," I say. I'm taken aback by this turn of events. I feel like I've just lost them both and I've only known Irina for a day and a half. They'll both be sucked into this massive fake operation that requires endless lies and double lives. They won't have time for me anymore. I'll be back in school, safe from harm but a million miles away from the action. I might hear about some bank president getting arrested and wonder if Strike and Irina had anything to do with it, but I won't know for sure. It was one thing to let Dale go back undercover without making a fuss, but to be reunited with both my birth parents and then have to stand back and watch them disappear into a world that has no place for me is something else.

"There's something else," says Strike.

"We don't want you to be part of what we do," says

Irina. "It's dangerous and it takes its toll. Look at what it's done to Strike."

"We want you with your family in Reindeer Crescent," says Strike. "That's where you belong."

I nod. I already picture myself trudging to school, standing in line for lunch, ignoring Brendan Chew. Not much fun.

"The thing is, though, you're really good," says Irina. "Nearly as good as I was when I started. Better than Strike."

"Have I said one mean thing to you?" says Strike, giving Irina an exasperated glare.

"He brings it out of me," shrugs Irina. "The way you pursued Vanessa. The fire in you. It would be such a waste to let that go."

Once again, I wasn't expecting this.

"What are you saying?" I ask.

"If a mission arises that involves a young person . . . ," Strike says.

"Someone who's a criminal or a potential victim," says Irina.

"Maybe you'd think about helping us out now and then?" says Strike.

I thought I was out and now it seems like I'm in. And way further in than I ever imagined. It means lying to my family and friends. But then, one of my family and most of my friends now know what I am, and I'm never telling Mom and Dad under any circumstances.

"So what do you think?" says Strike.

What do I think?

"I am not a spy," I tell them.

They both smile because they know only someone who is a spy would say something like that.

I smile, too, and then I head back to the concert, where the two skinny dudes are still on stage, strumming and whining their way through another classic from the Strangled Geese back catalog. I pass Little Lucien dancing with Alex, who has her eyes shut and is waving her arms in the air. Joanna sits alone at the end of an otherwise empty row of seats. I sit down next to her.

"This is literally the worst music anyone has ever made" are her first words to me.

"You can't clog-dance to it," I agree.

"K-Clog could," says Joanna.

I narrow my eyes at her. "Is that a challenge?" I ask. "Because Roxy is totally down for that."

"With her one leg?" mocks Joanna.

"One's all you need," I reply.

"Show me what you got," she says.

"You can't even begin to handle what I got" is my brilliant retort.

I didn't imagine my trip to New York would end with me fake clog dancing in a park with my best friend to the worst music anyone has ever made, but right now, there's nowhere else I'd rather be.

Coming soon . . .

# *Bridget Wilder*
# *Live Free,*
# *Spy Hard'*

"*F*aster, *Uber driver*," Joanna and I both scream at Jesse, whose only crime was his promptness in picking us up the second we fled the Reindeer Crescent Medical Center. Big Log got Joanna an Uber account in case of emergencies. She probably didn't think we'd be using it to rush to our school to stop a hypnotically suggested soccer player from letting a deadly wasp attack the First Lady of the United States of America and my sister, Natalie, the face of the Say Hello campaign. But if this doesn't qualify as an emergency, I don't know what does.

Jesse flinches as we scream at him, and he drives his little blue Mini Cooper toward our school as fast as it is capable of going on an unusually busy weekday morning. I texted Strike and Irina the shocking details of Klee's scheme, and I tipped off the local police that the dentist was a threat to the First Lady. If Jesse can't get us to the school on time, at least I know I've alerted reinforcements.

"You think T-shirt was under suggestion when he dated Nola?" Joanna asks, breaking my concentration. "She has insectoid features."

I give Joanna a pained look. Her face is still smeared with tomato sauce.

"Just trying to keep things light," she says. "We'll get there in time to save the most important woman on the planet. And also Jocelyn Brennan."

I laugh out loud at that. Joanna, it turns out, is fun to have around on spy missions.

She breaks into our catchy theme song: "Here come the spy twins on another adventure, here come the spy twins coming to your town. . . ." I join in for a reprise of the chorus.

"Uh-oh," says Jesse.

I stop singing as I see the reason for his *uh-oh*.

A police car signals us to pull over. Maybe they got Klee to confess? Maybe they want me to help them catch T-shirt? Maybe I'll get to ride in the cop car with the siren wailing!

Jesse stops his Mini Cooper and rolls down his window.

A uniformed cop leans inside and looks back at us. "Bridget Wilder?" he says.

"Did you get Klee to talk?" I ask, sounding brisk and businesslike, as if we're fellow law enforcers.

"Step out of the car for me, miss," says the cop.

I'm getting a ride in the police car!

I climb out. The cop peers down at me. "Dr. Klee made a complaint against you. He says you assaulted him, disrupted his place of business, and caused him emotional distress."

My mouth opens and closes. "He what . . . I what . . . he what?"

"I need you to come to the precinct."

"You're taking Klee's side?" I yelp. "Didn't you get my tip? He's a threat to . . ."

This is pointless. Whatever I say next will make me sound like a hysterical nut job. I nod sadly, lower my head, chew on my lip and put my hand in my pocket. I pull out a tissue to dab my eyes.

The officer is kind enough to wait for me to gather my emotions. This is a mistake on his part because, as I reached into my pocket, I also pulled out Klee's vial. I pop the lid and yell, "You're free, you monster, now *attack!*"

Nothing happens.

I shake the vial and a dead fly falls to the ground.

"*Klee!*" I howl in frustration.

"Get in the car," growls the officer. He takes a step toward me and then he freezes to the spot. His face reddens and he lets out a scream of pain.

The officer hops up and down on one foot. I stare at him in confusion and then I realize what just happened. He stood on the dead fly's transplanted stinger which, obviously, was lethal enough to pierce the leather of his cop shoes. Klee's reign of terror has claimed its first victim! I'm not sticking around to let him sting anyone else.

"Call 911," I yell at Joanna. "That cop's been stung by a marine wasp. He has a one in five chance of survival if treated quickly."

"One in *five?*" yells the cop. I probably shouldn't have said that out loud.

"What are you going to do?" says Joanna.

"Run!" I shout over my shoulder, as I take off toward the school.